THE
FAVOR

THE
FAVOR

MARCO A. RODRIGUEZ

Comprehensive editing by Alison Rodriguez
Copy Editing by Max Dobson of The Polished Pen
Cover Design by Rebecca Berto
www.bertodesigns.com
Interior design and formatting by:

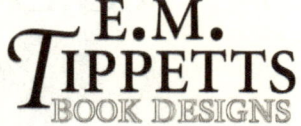

E.M.
TIPPETTS
BOOK DESIGNS
www.emtippettsbookdesigns.com

I want to dedicate this book to my wife, Alison and my son, Nathaniel.
I write this book in loving memory of Emil Rodriguez and Jaime Barreto.

CHAPTER
ONE

I can't sleep at all. I can't stop smiling. Even in the dark, I can see the shadow of my big dress hanging on the bathroom door. My ring shines through the darkest of places. I stick out my finger and gaze through the fractured light emanating from my tiny diamond.

What a night. Such a clear evening, unusually warm and windy for spring. I sit up and gaze upon my yard through the open window. The moon shines from above without a cloud in the sky. I get out of bed, tiptoe through the kitchen, and pick up the cordless phone. Opening the back door, I walk out to my yard. My old swing set sits in the middle, flowing gently in the breeze. I walk down the back steps, head over to the swings, and sit down on my rusty old set letting my weight settle on the grinding metal. Once the noise stops, I lift my bare feet from the plush grass, pull on the chains, and begin to swing back and forth. The warm breeze rustles my sheer nightgown. A few bright stars shine in the sky. I try hard not to swing too high. I just want to enjoy this night.

The cordless phone remains on my lap. Brian hasn't called all day. I left him messages, but he never called me back. I tried calling his mom, but she wasn't answering her phone. I know he is probably busy, but I want to at least hear his voice. I pull out the antenna on my phone and call him one more time.

His phone no longer rings and my call goes straight to voicemail. My heart drops a bit. I hear his voice.

"Hello, this is Brian. Leave a message," his phone says. The phone beeps.

"Brian, I know you told me to not bother you, but I haven't heard from you all day. Just call me back, please. I want to make sure that you are okay," I say.

I pull the phone away from my ear to hang up, but something comes to me.

"Do you remember the first time we kissed? We were around seven, I think. We were playing tag or something in the yard, and I was chasing you around my tree. You were always so much faster than I was and as hard as I tried I could never catch up to you.

"Anyway, just as I was about to give up, you suddenly slowed down as you were making that last turn around the tree. I quickly darted around the other side and then I caught you! For the first time ever, I caught you. The look on your face was priceless. I was so excited to finally have you that I lost my footing and we went tumbling to the ground. I remember holding on to you for dear life. I wasn't going to let you go.

"Somehow, I ended up on top of you. You pulled back, trying to break away from me. Then, out of the blue, you kissed me. It only lasted for a couple of seconds, but that's all you needed to distract me. You broke away and laughed as you ran out of the yard and down the street. I just sat there. Stunned. I had you and then just like that, you were gone.

"You eventually came back as if nothing happened. I never told you this, but when you ran off on me that day, I had this awful feeling that you were never going to come back." I pause for a moment. "But you did." I smile. "You did."

Hanging up, I push down the antennae on my phone. I'm tempted to go find him, as usual, but he told me not to bother him. It'll be okay. I know it'll be okay.

RACHEL GASPS loudly as she suddenly wakes up from her deep sleep. Her eyes gradually fixate on the ceiling fan hovering above her head, and she begins to slowly catch her breath. The constant clanking comforts her and she relaxes back down to the bed. The last few days have been a patchwork of strange dreams. As she begins to get a hold of her senses, she starts to hear other familiar sounds all around her: wind chimes from her neighbor's front porch, the bells from her church as they ring in the hour, and tree branches gently scraping the side of the house. She's just beginning to realize where she is: back home in her old bedroom.

As she lies in bed she hears other sounds: the dulcet tones of her mother rising above the din of clanking dishes, a bubbling coffee maker, and the subdued voices from others in the living room. It all sounds so muffled and distant. Although she can only pick out a few words here and there, she knows exactly what they are talking about. She can hear Uncle Fred and his very loud wife, Brenda, trying to be quiet but getting louder by the minute. Aunt Gracie barges in on the conversation as usual. There are other voices she can hear, but can't quite match the face to the voice.

Rachel takes a deep breath. She knows why they are all here. *They will just have to wait a little longer*, she thinks.

Lying on her old twin bed, she grimaces as her medication begins to slowly wear off. Some parts of her body are numb, while others throb in pain. After another deep breath, she tries to lift herself off the bed. Her body stiffens and she collapses into the mattress. No use. *What if I just stayed in bed?* She could just let the world pass her by. *That's too easy.* Even in her worst times, Rachel is not one to just lie in bed and give up. She needs to get up.

Like an old, defeated warrior, she gathers all of her strength and slowly pulls her weary body to a seated position. With her head down she sees her old pajamas hanging on her body. Looking around the room is like looking through a series of dull Polaroids of her past life. Her bedroom is completely frozen in time: the pink and white striped wallpaper, the worn finish on her bedside table, the faded pink curtains, and old personal knickknacks scattered around the room. A collage of stickers and magazine clippings of stars she idolized many years ago adorn the large, wooden-framed mirror over her dresser. Below the mirror her eyes land on an array of banners, ribbons, and certificates she had won as a child. It all meant so much to her once upon a time. *Funny how none of it matters now,* she thinks.

She moves to the edge of the bed, her feet gently touching the hardwood floor. The afternoon breeze tickles the back of her neck from the window next to her bed. From the many years of living in that room, she can tell the time of day just by looking at the angle of sunlight beaming through her window. Normally she wouldn't have slept in this late, but her internal clock is completely off. Family members chat and shuffle around in the kitchen, getting restless. Time to get ready for the day.

Pushing herself off the bed, she stands erect like a broken tree, spindly arms jutting out into the air. She slowly walks over to the mirror hanging above her dresser. She cocks her head and squints her eyes to take in the full image of her body's reflection. As if moving through molasses, she gently removes a small bandage under her hairline at her forehead. Reaching down into one of the drawers, she pulls out an old brush bursting with strands of hair. She begins to rake out her long, untamed hair then parts it to drape over her small wound. *I look so much older than thirty.*

She begins to make headway on her scraggly appearance until she glances at the mirror and sees a long garment bag hanging on the closet door. Turning, she walks over to the bag and reaches up to pull down the zipper, but instead yanks the bag off the door and throws it to the floor. She needs to leave. Right now.

Her bedroom door stands cracked open allowing light from the kitchen to filter into her room. When she was little her mother used to leave her door slightly ajar to keep an eye on her. That beam of light always made Rachel feel safe and protected. She derived comfort from hearing her mom cooking, cleaning, talking on the phone, or working while she slept surrounded by her stuffed animals.

Rachel peeks through the open door and sees everyone milling around in the kitchen and the dining room. Her mother ambles past her doorway and walks directly into her trophy room, chatting with family members as they admire different milestones and accomplishments from her past life. Rachel stifles the desire to call out for her mom and closes her bedroom door.

She heads back over to the dresser and yanks out an old green sweatshirt and a pair of outdated jeans way past their prime. Sitting back on her bed, she slowly takes off her pajamas and puts on the clothes. She picks up a hair tie and pulls her hair back in a quick ponytail letting her bangs cover her face. Walking over to the closet, she grabs an old pair of white sneakers and a long grey trench coat. She goes over to her desk in the corner of the room and pulls out a pen and piece of paper. Not hesitating for a second, she quickly writes down her thoughts. She folds the note and lays it on her bed then plucks her wallet from the nightstand and pulls out some money. As she throws her wallet back in the drawer, she notices her cracked cell phone and bent glasses. She drops the glasses on top of the nightstand and shoves the phone in the side pocket of her coat.

An old pair of dark-framed glasses she used to wear in high school sit in her dresser. She pulls them out, grabs a medicine bottle, takes two pills, and swallows them without water before she throws the bottle in her other pocket.

She steps over to the window by her dresser and lifts it wide open. With the small amount of strength still left in her body, she crawls out and jumps down to the grassy walkway in between her mother's house and the house next door. Walking casually on the pathway toward the front of the house, she crosses the neighbor's driveway and navigates her way through the parked cars to head down the street.

Moving at a quick pace, she walks a safe distance away and crosses the street to get a better view of her childhood home. She never realized, until now, how hard her Mom worked to make that house into a home. It was just the two of them. Her father was gone long before she was even born.

Her mom gave up so much for her. Pictures of her mother as a beautiful dancer used to fill the entire house when she was a little girl. She used to catch her mom gazing at some of her own portraits from time to time. Her mother rarely spoke of her past life. She had more important things to do, like take care of her gifted child—alone. Now her thirty-year-old daughter was running away.

Rachel's pace quickens down the street, but she has no idea where to go. *Just keep walking.* Many thoughts run through her head as she feels the medication kick in. She starts to slow down, desperately turning her head in every direction.

As she struggles to get her bearings straight, she runs into a person carrying several large department store bags. Rachel falls and looks up to see a tall, older woman dressed in a long grey evening coat and heels.

"Oh my God, I am *so* sorry!" Rachel scrambles over to the woman to check for any injuries. As she gets a better look, she slowly recognizes this smartly dressed woman.

"Mrs. Smith?!" Rachel asks in surprise. "Are you okay? I'm so sorry. I didn't see you there."

Mrs. Smith, whose body stiffened in response to the sudden physical contact, gets a better look at the person who collided into her. She takes a breath and smiles.

"Rachel. Oh my lord. What a surprise, dear. I didn't expect to see you," Mrs. Smith says as she brushes off her coat. "You seem to be in a bit of a hurry. Are you alright?"

"Yes, yes. I'm alright. Sorry again." Rachel smiles. "My mind was in another place. I didn't see you there..."

"That's quite all right, dear." Mrs. Smith carefully places her bags on the sidewalk and wraps her wiry arms around Rachel in a quick hug. Rachel returns the congenial gesture. "I didn't know you were back in town."

"I came down to visit my mom."

"That's good. So how is your mom doing?"

"Oh, um, she's doing very well, you know ... crazy as ever." Rachel snickers and throws her hands up in a melodramatic fashion.

Rachel has always maintained an arm's-length relationship with Brian's mom, but this is an extraordinarily awkward situation for both of them. From the corner of her eye, Rachel notices decorative balloons floating in the living room of Mrs. Smith's house. Rachel plays it off and continues the conversation without acknowledging the balloons. She does look quite beautiful, Rachel observes. It appears that Mrs. Smith was heading off to an evening event.

Mrs. Smith engages in small talk with Rachel as she stows the bags and her purse in the backseat of her car. She opens her front door with a not-so-subtle hint of wrapping up the conversation and making a quick getaway.

"You look great, Mrs. Smith," Rachel nods her head and smiles.

"Thank you, Rachel. I would have you come in for coffee or something, but I have somewhere to go."

"I can see that. Anywhere in particular?" Rachel asks.

Mrs. Smith squirms for a second but covers it up with a big smile. "A family affair, nothing special."

"Oh, ok. Please, don't let me stop you." Rachel steps away from the car as a wide, toothy grin breaks out on her face.

Mrs. Smith quickly exhales in relief and bends down to get into the car. She closes her car door and flashes her million dollar smile, once again.

"If you're still in town on Monday, please come by. I would love to catch up. I feel bad the way things ended with us," Mrs. Smith says.

"I don't even think about it much, to tell you the truth. All that nonsense is behind me. Don't think anything of it." Rachel pats the edge of the lowered car window and smiles reassuringly. "So I'll see you on Monday then?"

"Of course, dear," Mrs. Smith says with forced warmth in her voice.

Rachel turns to head back down the sidewalk, but whips around to Mrs. Smith. "How's Brian?"

Mrs. Smith inhales a sharp intake of air but quickly recovers. "Brian? Oh, well, he's fine, Rachel. He's doing well." She places her key in the ignition and starts the car.

"Oh, that's good. Please tell him I said hi, won't you?"

"Of course, dear."

Rachel's face beams with delight as she heads back down the street one more time. Mrs. Smith backs the car out of the driveway and waves to Rachel as she drives down the road. Rachel waves back at her former neighbor with enthusiasm as she strolls down the street. She keeps walking until Mrs. Smith's car disappears around the corner and out of sight. She runs back up the street a few feet away from Mrs. Smith's house and peers around a tree for any sign of the car. Once she realizes that the coast is clear, she crosses Mrs. Smith's yard and makes her way up the front steps.

Stopping at the front door, she looks through the bay window next to the entrance and rings the doorbell several times. When no one answers, she looks over her shoulder for any prying eyes. Seeing only an empty street, she reaches toward the plant sitting on the right side of the door, slips her hand under the flowerpot and pulls out a key. Rachel quickly unlocks the front door and enters the dwelling while closing the door behind her.

Exhaling, Rachel waits for her heartbeat to slow down to its normal pace as she leans back against the door. She can now add breaking and entering to her long list of sins. This is the house she and Brian played in so many years ago. It's been ten years and looking around it's definitely not the same house that she remembers. It is clear that Mrs. Smith has made many changes: fewer pictures on the walls, fewer personal items, fewer everything. The house stands as a functional domicile now, stripped of any warmth or familiarity. It suits her perfectly.

As she meanders through the house, she glances over at the large family portrait sitting on the wall over the fireplace: Mr. Smith and Mrs. Smith sitting on each side of a seven-year-old Brian, smiling as if they were the happiest family in the world. It was the last picture of Brian before the accident.

The only oddity in this sparsely decorated house was an arrangement of multi-colored balloons floating above a bouquet of flowers on the coffee table. Rachel walks slowly over to the arrangement, grabs one of the balloons, and reads the inscription out loud. "Congrats, Brian and Linda," she snorts. "Who the hell is Linda?"

Rachel searches for a note in the flowers or on the coffee table to find any more information about this Linda. Nothing. She walks over to the kitchen and rifles through the mail to uncover the truth. Nothing, again. She heads over to Mrs. Smith's bedroom and through the immaculate neatness finds nothing at all. Then she makes her way to Brian's old room.

Slowly opening the door, she turns on the lights. To her surprise his room looks exactly the way she remembers. His space, which still feels like him, stands in stark contrast from any other room in the house. The same bed, the same race car sheets, the same curtains, the same everything. Rachel finds it odd that Mrs. Smith would go to such lengths to change the look of the entire house, except for his room. His room hasn't been lived in for a long time and looks like a private museum that only Mrs. Smith can appreciate.

The only thing that stands out in this whole room is a small gift box wrapped neatly and placed in the middle of his twin-sized bed. She walks over to the gift and grabs the small card attached to it. She unfolds the card and says, "He's getting married. Brian is getting married to Linda." Rachel's body crumples on the bed in complete shock. She stares out into nothingness as she takes in this new information. Blinking away the tears that come, she takes a few deep breaths to regain her composure. The medication works its way to her head and suddenly the room starts spinning. She closes her eyes, breathes in and out deeply, and wipes the tears running down her face.

"No fucking way. He cannot get married. He can NOT get married. Not yet," Rachel whispers. She straightens up from her sloped position, rises from the bed, and begins looking around the room for more information. In a small garbage can by the dresser she pulls out an engraved invitation. After reading it she shoves it into her coat pocket and heads for the bedroom door.

On her way out of the room, Rachel notices a small wallet-sized picture on Brian's desk. She walks over and sees a shot of the two of them playing in the backyard. They must have been about seven years old at the time, and Mr. Smith took that picture while they were playfully hugging each other. She takes the picture, puts it in her coat, and quickly leaves the bedroom.

As she walks toward the front door, she notices a picture of Mr. Smith hanging in the hallway. In the picture Mr. Smith cradles Brian in his arms when he was just a little baby. She doesn't remember seeing that picture before and gazes upon the two of them for a moment, gently touching the portrait, as if to see if it were real. After that, she throws open the front door and leaves the house.

Walking down the sidewalk, Rachel heads for the busy intersection at the end of the street. When she gets to the corner, she raises her hand to wave down a cab. After a minute, a cab driver pulls over and stops next to her.

"The Buckingham Hotel," Rachel tells the driver, and he immediately takes off towards her destination. She begins to settle in her seat as the cab driver speeds through the early evening rush hour traffic. The quick stop-and-go motion of the cab causes her to become lightheaded.

"Slow down, please!" she yells at the driver.

"Alright," he snaps back. The cab starts slowing down as it heads into downtown. She begins to slip deeper and deeper into her seat, fighting off the nausea roiling in her belly. She rolls down the window to let the cool breeze calm her anxious soul. Traffic begins to move more smoothly, but from her seated position she can only see the sky and the tops of buildings flying past her. She closes her eyes. There is no doubt in her mind that she needs to see Brian. Everything else can wait. She falls in and out of consciousness throughout the remainder of the trip.

"Ma'am? Ma'am? We're here! Wake up, ma'am!" the driver yells.

Rachel rouses with a start. "We're here?" she whispers with a raspy voice.

"Yes, ma'am." The cab driver turns to face her in the back seat. "Your head is bleeding, ma'am!" Rachel sits up and looks at her reflection in the rearview mirror. A small amount of blood trickles down the side of her face from underneath her hairline.

"Damn it," she says to herself, regretting her decision to take the bandage off before she left her mother's house.

"Don't bleed all over my cab, ma'am!"

"I'm not going to! Give me some tissues, please," Rachel barks as she uses her sleeve to stem the flow.

The cabbie quickly grabs a few tissues from his dispenser up front and hands them to her in the backseat. As he gives her the tissues, Rachel hands the cab driver some cash from her pocket.

"Is it enough? I can't tell." Rachel applies the tissue to her forehead.

"Yes, but please, not all over my cab."

"Alright! Alright!" She quickly gets out of the cab and the car speeds off. Taking a few steps onto the sidewalk, Rachel looks around and realizes that he dropped her off at the wrong spot. "Hey! Wait!" she yells to the cabbie, but he's already gone.

She recognizes the area and starts walking the three blocks to the hotel through a sea of people rushing to get home. Momentarily she thinks about grabbing another cab, but with so many people hailing taxis at the same time she decides to walk.

Rachel tries to keep up with the frenzied pace of people rushing to get home, but ends up getting bumped relentlessly by pedestrians passing her on the sidewalk. Her staggered steps begin to get worse, and she decides to pull off into a tiny alley between two large buildings. Light snowflakes begin to fall around her as she collapses against a wall sliding down to the ground in a hard fall. Her vision becomes blurry as she tries stay conscious and stop the bleeding from her head. Items from her pockets fall out as she takes a tumble. On the ground she tries to retrieve all of the items, including the picture of her and Brian. She sits up and looks at the picture for a moment. Within seconds everything around her starts spinning and she slides back down to the ground.

"Brian!" she whispers to herself and with a few quick breaths she passes out.

CHAPTER
TWO

I stand on a chair in my bedroom, wearing my beautiful wedding dress as Mom tries to stitch the dress in tighter around my waist. My mother and I have been arguing over little things throughout the morning while Aunt Brenda busies herself taking pictures of me in my dress.

"Mom, don't bring it in too much," I say.

"Why did you go and lose more weight?"

I don't know why she's fussing about the dress. So, it's a little big. I didn't expect to lose more weight than I—

"Ouch!" I yelp as the needle pricks me in my side. My mom told me she used to alter her own dresses while touring with the National Dance Company. Maybe she wasn't very good.

"You keep squirming. Stop moving around so much," Mom grumbles.

"Aunt Brenda, please tell your sister that I will need all of my blood to walk down the aisle. If she keeps pricking me, I'll faint from blood loss before I even reach the priest." I can't see my aunt, but I can hear her chuckle as her camera clicks away.

"Sylvie, give the girl a break," laughs Aunt Brenda. Sylvie. What a funny name. I only hear it when Aunt Brenda whisks into town for a quick visit. Neither mom nor my aunt liked her real name, Sylvia. Shortening the name made it a little easier to handle.

"Ouch! Mom!" I jerk away from her.

"I told you to stop squirming," Mom says. "Just a few more minutes and we'll be done. Alright?"

"We're going to be late for the wedding!"

"Honey, the ceremony is not until four. It's only 8:30 in the morning. The dress hangs on you like a bag. I need to put some shape in it."

I wince at that last comment. I grew up as flat as an ironing board and now, at nineteen, I still haven't filled out yet. Maybe by the time I'm thirty ...

"Did you hear from Brian yesterday?" Mom asks sweetly.

"No, Ma. He told me not to bother him."

Mom breaks away from stitching my waist and looks up at me. "Honey, are you sure he's coming? You know how he is."

"It's our wedding day, Mom. Brian wouldn't do that, not on our wedding day. Besides, his mom is paying for most of it."

Aunt Brenda puts down her camera and sits in the chair across from me. "Rachel, do you remember the first time you met Brian?"

"In preschool," Mom jumps in as she resumes working on my dress.

She was right. She was exactly right. I remember that day very well.

My mother, the strong and beautiful Sylvia Stein, breezes into my room and wakes me up with a few playful kisses on my forehead. That had to be the sweetest way for a four year old to wake up, but I was already up of course. I can remember the sun shining brightly through my window. My mom, dressed in office attire for her secretarial job, had cereal and sliced apples waiting for me. With the strength of a thousand men, she lifts me out of the avalanche of books surrounding my bed and whisks me over to the kitchen to eat.

After breakfast, I run to my bedroom to get dressed and brush my teeth on my own, as usual. I had always been a good little soldier for my mom. She always talked to me like a little adult, no cute baby talk from her. I didn't have a dad *around, so I always used to say 'it's just me and my mom'. Honestly, I think that's the way my mom preferred it. Me too.*

We get into her car and drive to my very first day of preschool. Mom holds my hand as we make our way through the myriad of parents and kids moving from one set of toys to another. Whenever my mom and I were out running errands, I would hold on to her hand with all of my might. She was my hero and my protector, and I never, ever thought I would let go of her hand. I always felt her strength and love flow through me from her fingertips. Her grip was never too tight, just firm and resolute, like she was.

As I walked through the school holding my mom's hand, I saw him for the very first time. In the middle of a sea of laughing kids stood a little boy wearing a dark blue sweater and brown corduroys. He was just standing there not playing with any of the other kids or with any of the toys in the room. Under his dark mop of hair I could see that he looked really sad, like he had just been crying.

Unbelievably, I let go of my mom's hand and walked over to him. He raised his head and looked into my eyes for a long time. He smiled, and then I smiled as well. It was like we were long lost friends.

"Wanna race?" I ask. "Ready, set, go!" I scream, racing away from him. I remember running my heart out, laughing and screaming for no reason at all. I looked back and saw him chasing me, cackling and screeching the whole way too. We raced around the classroom, knocking things over, being very loud and rambunctious. With a strong voice, our preschool teacher firmly tells us to stop running.

I don't listen, though. I keep running and laughing until a tall figure steps into my path. I look up and see this thin, pretty woman with wild red hair and a flowered dress to match. She folds her arms and shoots Brian a very stern look. He stops in his tracks and all fun ended in that moment. I could tell that she was a force to be reckoned with.

Yes, I remember the first day we met like it was yesterday.

"You know, Brian hasn't been the same since his dad died," Mom says.

"Did you have to mention that today, Mom?"

"You know it's true, dear."

Of course it's true. She just doesn't have to keep reminding me, though.

"Ouch!" I scream. Those damn needles.

RACHEL SLOWLY opens her eyes, takes a deep breath, and begins to look around through the falling snow. *Maybe I was only out for a few minutes.* She pats her head to see if it is still bleeding. Pulling her hand away, she finds it dry.

Pushing against the alley wall, she eases into a standing position surrounded by a dusting of snow. She shakes the cobwebs from her head and with one hard intake of air she continues on to her destination. Rachel enters the hotel through the large sliding doors and steps into the grand foyer. She is taken aback by the elegance surrounding her—bright ivory marble floors and columns interspersed with large floral arrangements around the room. The pristine lobby reminds her of a grand old library with an Art Deco feel.

Out of the blue she starts feeling a little out of place. From every angle she finds well-dressed tourists lounging in comfy chairs, planning their adventures in the city. A constant bustle of people in business attire enter and exit the hotel making the lobby a high-traffic area. She glances over at the bar full of TGIF bliss from workers winding down from the week.

Rachel stands in the foyer a moment trying to figure out her next step. Out of the corner of her eye, she sees a woman wearing a dark business suit walking up to her.

"Mrs. Benson?" she asks with a smile in her voice. Rachel slowly turns toward the tall, bubbly brunette wearing a nametag: Laura.

"Mrs. Benson? Um, no," Rachel replies politely with a smile.

"Oh, I'm so sorry. I am expecting someone. Did you need any help?"

"Um, well, I *am* looking for the Smith and LaRusche wedding rehearsal. My invitation said it is here, but I can't find the ballroom," Rachel says. The woman's face lights up in delight.

"Oh, you're with Brian and Linda's wedding party! That's great. Their rehearsal is up in the Grand Ballroom on the fourth floor," the woman answers. "You're a bit early. The rehearsal is not for a few hours."

"Oh …" Rachel looks off into the lobby, not quite sure what to do next.

"I'm the Event Manager for their wedding. Oh, sorry, I'm Laura." She chuckles and extends her hand to Rachel. "Completely forgot to introduce myself. That happens every once in awhile."

"Nice to meet you." Rachel smiles politely and shakes her hand. "Have you known the happy couple very long?"

"I've only met them once when they came to do their site visit last year, but I've worked with Linda for almost a year on the arrangements. She's so sweet."

"Last year? Wow, they've been engaged that long?"

"Today will be three years to be exact. They wanted to have their wedding date on the anniversary of their engagement."

"Oh wow. How lovely." Rachel's eyes dart around the room searching for a quick exit.

"Like a storybook wedding …" Laura looks off with a dreamy smile.

"Yeah, right." Rachel cuts Laura off. "You did say the ballroom was on the fourth floor?"

"Yes, the elevator is down the hall. They're just setting up so you're more than welcome to wait at the bar instead of a big, empty ballroom for the next few hours," Laura says.

"I don't mind waiting in the ballroom, if that's alright with you."

"Yes, of course. Please, be my guest!"

"Thanks."

"I would take you up there myself, but I need to wait here for my client."

"No, I understand. I'll find my way."

"You can't miss it. Their engagement portraits are being displayed throughout the Grand foyer right now. It looks terrific."

"Wow. Wish I had thought of that," Rachel snorts under her breath.

"I'm sorry?" Laura asks.

"Nothing." Rachel straightens up and flashes an innocent grin.

"I'll be up there when the rest of the wedding party arrives. Page me on the house phone if you need anything," Laura says and walks briskly away.

Rachel heads for a bank of elevators to her left. She pushes the UP button and after a short wait, the doors open and she enters. As she stands in the elevator, the mirrored walls give Rachel an unexpected view of herself from all sides: a slender, disheveled woman in a long, grey coat with greasy hair pulled back into a ponytail, jagged bangs on her forehead, and large brown glasses on her face. Rachel never felt pretty at any point in her life, but at that moment she thinks she's hit the pinnacle of unattractiveness. She closes her eyes as the elevator makes it to the fourth floor.

As she steps out into the lobby area of the Grand Ballroom, she spots several digital signage boards displaying the upcoming event in the Lexington Ballroom.

"Congratulations, Brian and Linda" appear all throughout the lobby monitors. Then their engagement picture pops up all at the same time. She walks over to see the spectacle and giggles. *Kind of freaky,* she thinks.

"Congratulations, Brian and Linda", she says quietly to herself. She patiently waits for the portrait of both of them to reappear. Then the picture arrives. She takes a good look. Brian hasn't really changed that much, other than wearing glasses and putting on a little bit of weight. The one thing she notices is that he's smiling. He's smiling from ear to ear in all of the pictures. With his arms wrapped around her, he kisses Linda in each picture, as if he is really in love with her. Rachel has never seen that side of Brian before, not even when they were together.

Brian was never a person to smile for any picture. She clearly remembers that piece of history. Getting him to smile for anything was such a chore. Much to the chagrin of his parents, Brian refrained from smiling in any of his old pictures from school. You'd have to go to the days before second grade to see a smiling, laughing young boy. She remembers that part of Brian the best. That was the sweetest, most innocent time in their lives. Just like that picture she grabbed from Brian's dresser. Those beautiful moments didn't last very long, though.

She walks over to an ornate bench in the foyer facing the entire row of wall monitors. With the little strength she has left, Rachel slowly eases herself down to the plush seat. As she gets comfortable she pulls out the picture that she took from Brian's room. Holding the picture in her hand, she tries to relive that moment. She and Brian were about four years old, sitting on a playground bench next to their preschool. The old film processing makes the picture look dated, but it remains a true artifact of their lives. Right there, he's smiling without a care in the world.

Rachel sighs as she looks at the picture. It reminds her of a terrific time they had together when they were kids. From the first day of preschool, they were absolutely inseparable. He would go do his own thing and Rachel followed. During their early years they were the cutest, most adorable best friends anyone had ever seen. They went to each other's birthday parties, field trips, beach outings, cookouts, etc. Their mothers also became the best of friends since Rachel and Brian spent so much time together. There are thousands of pictures and hundreds of hours of video of just the two of them. Their pictures were plastered all over each other's home. All of the holidays were spent in each other's houses. Both moms took turns babysitting the other child when alone time was needed. The moms also broke up many a battle between the two, but they were always able to keep the peace. The moms were both very strict with regard to their manners, cleaning up after themselves, and taking personal responsibility as young children. In spite of the myriad of rules, Rachel and Brian had so much fun with each other.

Those early years were the greatest ever for Rachel. Until the accident.

CHAPTER
THREE

I sit on the coffee table in the living room wearing my fully-completed wedding dress. I am just sitting there staring out into space, listening to my mom and my aunt fuss about something or another. Then I can hear my mom's soft steps sink into the plush carpet as she walks up quietly behind me.

"You know, honey, you do look beautiful," she says. I turn around to see my mom fighting back tears and I smile from ear to ear.

I get up and turn around to let her get a good look at the best work of her life. I do see a tear or two rolling down her cheek. I was waiting for those tears to come. Walking over to my mom, I give her a small hug. She wraps her arms around me and grabs on for dear life. My mom, she feels so tiny in my arms. What a great mom.

She pulls away trying to take one more look at her only child.

"Now, you fill out that dress quite well," she says. "You used to always wear those baggy, unflattering clothes." She smiles. "You've turned out to be such a beautiful woman."

I smile, and blink away my tears. "Mom, stop it. You're going to make me smear my makeup." I pick up a napkin from the coffee table and dab away the *flow of tears that I didn't expect to shed so early. My mom comes up to me, holds both my hands, and takes one more look at me.*

"You're so beautiful, Rachel. I dreaded this day for years because I knew someday that I was going to have to say good-bye to my little girl. You're not my little girl anymore." She begins to cry. I embrace her again, trying not to make this a tear fest.

"You know I'll always be your little girl, right, Mommy?" I whisper in her ear.

She grabs me tighter than ever before. "I know. I know," she tearfully whispers. Wow, she never grabbed on to me this hard before. I think I'm going to pass out.

All of a sudden I hear the clicking of a camera. I look up to see my aunt Brenda taking snapshots of us. We separate for a moment. My mom takes her hand to wipe the tears from my face.

"Beautiful," Aunt Brenda says. "Come on, just a few more." She tries to persuade us to pose for more pictures, but I think my mom has had enough.

"Well, the car is not going to pick us up for another couple of hours. We shouldn't have put the dress on so early," Mom says.

"Oh please," my aunt says with a smile as she walks back to the kitchen.

Mom walks me over to the couch and sits me down. "I know this is a very important day for you, but there are some things we need to discuss." Mom takes a breath. "You know, about your wedding night ..." she says with trepidation. Oh boy, I've got to cut this short right now.

"Mom, I know what you're going to say. I know you feel that it's your duty to have this conversation with me," I take a deep breath. "I just want to let you know that I don't really need it."

Mom looks up at me in confusion. "What do you mean?"

"I mean, it's 1989, Mom. I have all the information. I'm okay with what's going to happen on my wedding night. I get it, really." I pat her hand reassuringly.

Mom jerks her hand away from mine. "Get it? Get what? What's that supposed to mean?"

"What I mean is that, I'm good. I get it. I'm good. I'll be completely fine. Really."

Then mom gives me this weird look.

"You've done it already, haven't you!"

My mouth hits the floor. "What? You can't ask me that!"

Mom squints her eyes. "Well, is it true?"

"Mom, I can't tell you if I did it or not."

"Why not? I'm your mother."

I can tell that this conversation is going to end badly, so I get up and walk towards the living room windows. As much fun as that conversation could have been, I have other things on my mind. Mom sits in silence for a few moments and lets out a long sigh.

"Did you hear from Brian this morning?" she asks.

"No."

FROM HER bench Rachel hears rustling in the ballroom. She slowly picks herself up, heads through the foyer, and walks through the large double doors of the Grand Ballroom.

What a beautiful ballroom, she thinks. She didn't expect it to be this nice. A large chandelier dangles from the ceiling in the center of the room. Wall columns stand in all four corners of the ballroom with large, elegant artwork hanging throughout. A bride could lose herself twirling around the center of this magnificent room.

Nothing in the room is laid out yet. No chairs, no stage, nothing. Rachel looks around but there is nowhere to sit. The lights in the ballroom are dimmed leaving the space feeling pretty empty and quiet. She doesn't know what to do next.

All of a sudden the lights in the room spring to life. Rachel turns towards the front of the room and sees a pony-tailed woman walking briskly towards her. Casually dressed in jeans and a purple T-shirt, she approaches Rachel so quickly that she has no time to react. Rachel just stands there and waits for the impact.

"Are you Tracy," she angrily asks in a very heavy Polish accent.

"Um, no."

She waves her hands wildly. "Well, do you know where she is?"

"No, because I don't know who this Tracy is, or who you are for that matter." Rachel says calmly.

"Who are you?" She steps in closely to get a better look at her prey.

"I'm with the wedding party," Rachel replies.

The woman's irascible demeanor quickly melts away. "Oh my God, I am so sorry. I didn't mean to speak to you that way. I am so sorry," the lady says in a quivering voice. "I am expecting a couple of ladies from the agency. I am so sorry. I just assumed from what you are wearing ... I got confused."

"Don't worry about it, Miss ..." Rachel tries to get her name.

"Malinda. Just Malinda," she says. "I'm with the florist."

"Oh, ok. I couldn't help but notice ... you have a Polish accent?"

"Yes, I am from Lublin—"

"Oh, just east of Warsaw?" Rachel asks. Malinda lights up.

"Yes. Have you been there?"

"No. Dowiedziałem się o Polsce ze szkoły," Rachel says.

Malinda laughs. "So you speak Polish?"

"Bardzo mało," Rachel says with a smile.

"Very little, huh? Well you speak it very well."

"Thanks. It just comes out from time to time." Rachel learned several different languages in school, but she picked up Polish from her childhood piano teacher who had been a recent immigrant from Krakow. By nature, Rachel was always shy, but she came out of her shell when speaking to someone in a different language.

As Rachel and Malinda chat away, two ladies walk in from the back of the ballroom. Malinda exhales and smiles.

"I think it's them." Malinda turns away and jogs towards the women. "It was nice talking to you," she says over her shoulder.

As Malinda meets with the women, Rachel hears large items tumbling to the floor. She turns to see a handful of guys arguing with each other as they pick up stacks of white chairs scattered across the floor. Rachel walks over to the bickering men who stop all activity as she draws near.

"Hello," one of the men says in broken English.

"Hola. Son ustedes bien?" Rachel asks. The men all smile.

"Grand?" asks one of the men.

"Sí, esta es la sala correcta," Rachel replies.

"Gracias, señora," one of the men politely replies. The men immediately start laying out the chairs in the ballroom. Just then a group of hotel housemen roll in sections of staging for the ceremony. From the corner of her eye, she can see another vendor entering the room. It looks like the ballroom is starting to get busy. She wants to get out of the way.

Rachel walks over to the men setting up the chairs and grabs one.

"Discúlpeme. ¿Puedo considerar una de las sillas, por favor?" Rachel asks. The men gladly nod yes.

"Gracias." Rachel pulls the chair to the back of the room and sits down. Watching the room getting set up gives her a chance to take a breather. Finally able to get slightly comfortable for the first time in days, she smiles. Seeing everyone work together to make a couple's dream come true allows her to forget her own world for a little while.

Just then Laura, the Event Manager, walks into the ballroom, sees Rachel sitting in the back of the room, and heads over to her.

"Hi. So sorry I wasn't able to come up sooner. Are you doing okay up here?" Laura asks as she leans down to Rachel.

"Oh yes. I enjoy seeing the place come to life."

"Good, good. I'm sorry, I didn't get your name earlier."

"Rachel. It's Rachel."

"Rachel. Thanks. Well, I just finished with my client and wanted to see if you needed anything. Also, I just got off the phone with Linda and she said that they're running a little behind schedule. I mentioned to her that you had arrived, but she was confused since most of the wedding party is with her right now," Laura says.

"Let her know that I'm a friend of Brian's. I was just visiting from out of town when his Mom invited me to come to the rehearsal. I wanted to come down to offer my congratulations," Rachel replies.

"Oh that's nice." Laura checks her phone briefly. "Are you sure you don't need anything? I have another meeting in ten minutes."

"I'm alright," Rachel says. Laura smiles and speeds off to talk to one of the vendors.

One of the men setting the chairs in a row next to Rachel looks over in her direction. He notices something running down her forehead.

"Disculpe señora, usted tiene algo corriendo por su frente?" the man asks Rachel. She takes her hand and touches her forehead. It's wet. Her forehead is bleeding.

Rachel immediately gets up and heads for the foyer. After a quick look around she makes a beeline for the nearest bathroom. She rushes over to the sink, picks up a handful of paper towels, and presses them against her head to stop the bleeding. Then she runs water over a few more towels and swaps out the bloody ones for clean ones.

A few minutes pass and she stems the flow of blood and washes her face clean of any residue. She applies pressure to the wound with a few extra towels and walks over to a bench in the lobby of the bathroom.

As she rests, she catches sight of a blurry reflection in the bathroom mirror. She left her glasses on the counter after washing her face. Even without glasses Rachel is unimpressed with what she sees.

"Oh my God," she whispers, removing the tissue from her forehead to get a better look. With or without glasses, Rachel was never happy with her looks. *The blurry appearance is an improvement*, she thinks. She reapplies the tissue to her head and leans back against the wall, closing her eyes.

After about twenty minutes or so, Rachel gingerly makes her way out of the bathroom and heads back to the ballroom. As she walks past the doors, the sight of the elegant arena completely takes her breath away. Sharp rows of linen-covered chairs stand on each side of a center aisle that leads to a stage draped in white velour curtains. Sheer white fabric dangles from the center chandelier out to the side of the ballroom. Opulent vases line the aisle as the lighting crew finishes setting up the room. *Is this Heaven?* she wonders.

She steps further into the ballroom and notices one of the housemen unplugging his cell phone from the wall.

"Is that for a Nokia phone?" Rachel asks as she approaches him.

"Yes."

"May I plug in my phone? I have no juice and left my charger at home."

"Sure." He hands her the charger.

"Thanks." Rachel plucks her phone from her pocket, plugs it in, and heads back to the ceremony set.

Rachel walks behind the last row of chairs and glides halfway down the aisle, as if she were the bride. Stopping, she looks back at the entrance of the ballroom, slides sideways towards the closest chair and sits down, staring at the stage.

Sitting in her chair without looking at the ballroom doors, she is too tired and in too much pain to think about anything else but seeing Brian. Just the idea of him getting married is hard enough. She closes her eyes and hopes it all works out.

CHAPTER
FOUR

I t's a couple of hours before the wedding, but my mom felt we needed to have a family reunion at the house before heading to the church. Here I am trying to not ruin my hideously puffy dress while my mom serves coffee and snacks to my extended family.

I carefully sit in the kitchen and watch her act the perfect hostess. She is actually pretty good at it considering all of those years she worked at a restaurant. Just to keep a roof over our heads, she'd work her day job as a secretary during the week and a waitress on the weekends. At just five-two inches, she's the tiniest woman I know, but the strongest person I have ever met. She had to be. All this time it was just Mom taking care of everything. No one else.

And here she is showing off the place to Grandma and Grandpa, and all the little kids. My grandparents are in the Trophy Room marveling at all of my academic awards, including my State Spelling Bee Championship ribbon and my trophy for winning Top Talented Teen. I received so many accolades when I was young, my mom had to transform her sewing room into an area showcasing all of my work.

Aunt Brenda stands in the living room, serving tea to Aunt Anna and Uncle

Bill who sits alongside his wife, Agatha. Aunt Anna and Uncle Bill have never been to our house. My mom and I used to visit them in Brooklyn when I was little.

One by one my family members stroll over to sit by me at the kitchen table. Oh boy. I'm not in the mood to talk, but I can hardly move in this dress. I prepare myself to sit and endure.

"So Brian must be very excited," my aunt Anna says as she slides in the chair next to me.

"Oh yes, very," I reply.

"Is this the boy you have been chasing around all these years?" Uncle Bill pipes in. Mom swats his arm in response.

"Yeah, something like that," I say.

"So, I heard you skipped college to get married," Uncle Bill says as he leans back in his chair. Oh boy, that didn't take very long. Here comes the Inquisition.

"Well, it's only a temporary thing, Uncle Bill."

"Is it money you need?" he quickly asks.

"No, Uncle Bill." I'm drowning. With every passing second, I am drowning.

"Rachel received several scholarships already, Bill. She just decided not to go," Mom glances at me with a smile. Everyone turns to her in surprise.

It's nice seeing my mom stand up for me. She did not react so calmly when I told her my decision, but she seems okay with it now.

"Like I said, it's only a temporary thing. Once the wedding is over, Brian and I will figure out our next step."

"Is Brian going to college?" Aunt Anna asks.

"No, he just wants to continue with his music," Mom interjects.

"What kind of music?" Uncle Bill asks.

"It's uh ... heavy metal," I reluctantly confess.

"Heavy metal?" Grandpa suddenly jumps in. "What the hell is that? I hear that all the time in the car and all over the place. That's not music. That's garbage."

"Yes, Grandpa, it's garbage." I put my hands over my face. Maybe I can disappear for a few minutes so they can have this argument without me.

"Leave the girl alone," Grandma says. "This is her special day. Give her a little

peace." *Grandma gets up to grab more tea, but kisses me on the forehead before she walks over.*

Everyone gets up from the kitchen table and heads to the dining room for more snacks, except for Mom. I don't even have to look at her. She has this way of just staring into my soul until I break. I guess you can call it one of her super powers. I give in. I turn toward her and smile.

"You okay?" she asks.

"I'm fine, Mom. Just a little uncomfortable."

"I wish you had waited to put on that dress," she frowns.

"How were you going to have time to alter the dress if we had waited?"

"I've altered many a dress in my day, dear. I did it at home when I was a little girl and throughout my entire time with the Company. I used to fix everyone's outfits. Especially the girls that wanted a little help with their dresses before they went out. I tried to teach you, but you didn't want to learn. Funny, how you are so smart in many subjects, but a needle and thread make you scream and pull your hair out." She gets me to smile a bit. She was right. I hated sewing and she wanted me to learn it so badly.

"Maybe I'll pick up a needle and thread when I have my first child, alright?"

"We'll see." She smiles before sipping her coffee.

We'll see.

RACHEL SLEEPS soundly in her chair waiting for everyone to arrive. As she dozes a young, beautiful brunette surrounded by a handful of women walk up the aisle towards her. She breaks away from the women and gently taps the sleeping interloper on the shoulder.

Rachel wakes up. Immediately opening her eyes, she sits up and takes in the young brunette standing in the aisle poring over her.

"I'm sorry, miss. Do I know you?" the young lady asks with a smile.

Rachel scoots up in her chair and pulls down her shirt. "Sorry, I didn't mean to nod off like that."

"That's ok. I think you might be in the wrong ballroom. Let me call my event manager to check."

"This *is* Brian and Linda's wedding rehearsal, correct?" Rachel asks.

"Well, yes, I'm Linda."

Rachel slowly recognizes the woman from the digital monitors in the foyer and stands up. "Hi, Linda. It's nice to finally meet you. My name is Rachel. I'm a good friend of Brian's." Linda squints her eyes and moves back from Rachel. "I am a childhood friend of his. We go way back. Our mothers were best friends. We went to school together and I know it's last minute, but I happened to be in town—"

Rachel doesn't even get a chance to finish as Linda flashes a huge smile and wraps Rachel in a big hug. Caught off guard, Rachel returns the hug awkwardly. They break after a few moments.

"Oh my gosh. It's so nice to meet you, Rachel! Brian told me that he didn't have any friends back when he was in school." Linda holds her hands warmly.

"Well, like I said, we go way back. We separated after high school."

"Really? When did you two meet?"

"Preschool. After we became best friends our moms became friends. We spent most of our childhood together."

"Oh that's so sweet! How did you find out about the wedding rehearsal?" Linda finally releases Rachel's hands.

"His mom told me. I was visiting my mom and ran into her on my way out—"

Linda shrieks with joy and envelops Rachel in another hug. The other ladies that entered the room with Linda encircle the two and chat quietly.

"Ladies, this is Rachel. She's a childhood friend of Brian's. She happened to be in town and was nice enough to come by and say hi." Linda says. "Rachel, I want you to meet Raquel, Mandy, Kari, Lucy, Becky ..." There are way too many bridesmaids for Rachel to remember so she simply waits for Linda to finish prattling off the names. "These are my bridesmaids," Linda continues as Rachel and the ladies exchange handshakes. "The rest of the pack is stuck in traffic, with that crazy snow coming down. We should see them within an hour or so. Brian is going to flip when he sees you."

"Oh yeah, he's definitely going to flip." Rachel says under her breath as she turns away to look around the room.

"Do you think you can make the wedding tomorrow? I have a couple of extra seats available and we would love to have you. I haven't been able to invite anyone on Brian's side, except for his relatives."

"Um … that's terribly sweet, but I don't know. I don't have much time and I just came by to say hi …"

Linda's face falls in a hangdog expression.

"I live in Seattle now and I'm just here to visit family. I have to fly out later tonight. Brian and I have lost touch over the years so I didn't even know he was getting married. If I had known, I would have made arrangements."

"Oh, okay. I understand." She nods her head with a crestfallen look in her eyes.

"I'm sure you already know this, but Brian is not exactly the *'hey, let's keep in touch'* kind of guy. He's not very social. Not his fault, though. Just the way he is." Rachel shrugs with a smile.

"Yeah, you're right." Linda chuckles. "It's amazing he had any friends at all."

"Oh, he had a few … including a girlfriend or two," Rachel says.

Linda's head jerks back mid-chuckle. "Really? He never told me about any of his past girlfriends."

"Yeah, he's not very forthcoming about a lot of things. Besides, those girls were losers anyway."

Linda sniggers in response to that last comment. "Please don't leave. Would you stay at least for the rehearsal? Brian's due here any minute and we're planning to have drinks afterwards."

"I only came here to say hi to him. He's not quite expecting me," Rachel says.

"I know he would love to see you. I can have my limo take you to the airport or wherever you need to go. It's on me," Linda says. *What a super nice girl,* Rachel thinks. *She seems so genuinely sweet. How could I possibly say no?*

"Well, okay. If I have time, I would love to stick around for a couple of drinks," Rachel says and Linda gives her another big hug.

"That's wonderful. I can't wait to see the expression on his face when he sees you here."

"Oh, I'm sure he will be very surprised."

"I would love to stay and chat some more, but I have to get this rehearsal thing going. I have a small snack buffet set up in the other room. Please help yourself." Linda turns to see Laura the Event Manager and her assistants enter the ballroom. "Thanks for coming, Rachel."

"It's my pleasure," Rachel says.

Linda jaunts off to assign jobs to Laura, as well as her bridesmaids. Rachel walks out of the ballroom into the foyer and takes a quick glance at the happy couple on the electronic board by the entrance. A couple of hotel housemen place a few poster-sized portraits of Brian and Linda on easels around the foyer, turning the whole area into their own personal museum. She's sure this wasn't Brian's idea.

Behind her Rachel hears the doors of the elevator fly open. A number of men laugh and talk amongst themselves as they exit the elevator and head for the ballroom. Without turning around, she stands still, listening for Brian's voice. She stares straight ahead as a group of young men dressed in sleek business casualwear stroll right past her. Out of the corner of her eye, she sees that all of the men are clean-shaven and fit, but one of the men turns back to chat with one of the other guys. *It's him,* she thinks. He looks healthier and better dressed than she remembers. *He looks very handsome too.*

Rachel turns towards the men as they walk into the ballroom. *His mom must still be on her way.* She walks slowly toward the entrance of the room, but does not enter. She peeks inside and sees Brian walk over and give Linda a warm hug and kiss. The rest of the men sidle around the space, laughing and joking with each other. She doesn't remember Brian having that many male friends. Then she sees Brian doing the meet and greet with everyone, shaking hands, laughing and patting people on the back. This is not the Brian she knew all those years ago. This is the new and improved Brian.

Never in her wildest dreams did Rachel think she would one day attend Brian's wedding rehearsal with a different bride. She watches Brian looking so happy, relaxed, and at peace with himself. He was such an introvert when they were growing up together, but now it looks like he's the life of the party. *Maybe his mom was right those many years ago,* Rachel thinks. Maybe she WAS the one that made it difficult for Brian to grow and create his own life. She never dreamed that he could turn out to be such an outgoing, handsome person.

"Rachel?!" She hears a very familiar voice coming up behind her. Rachel knows exactly who that voice belongs to and slowly turns around. Mrs. Smith stands frozen in her spot carrying those same department store bags she had outside of her house. Rachel flashes Mrs. Smith her toothiest grin.

"Mrs. Smith. How are you?" Rachel asks sweetly.

"What are you doing here?" Mrs. Smith's eyes widen in surprise.

"What do you mean? I was just in the neighborhood—"

"I know what you're doing here." Mrs. Smith presses her thin lips together and narrows her eyes.

"Enlighten me. What am I doing here?" Rachel asks innocently, clasping her hands.

"This isn't the right time to do all of this."

"Do what? I'm not doing anything."

Mrs. Smith takes a breath and steadies her voice. "Listen, Rachel, the past is the past. Brian is very happy with Linda."

"Oh, I know. I had a very nice chat with the future Mrs. Brian Smith. She does seem very nice," Rachel says.

Mrs. Smith's face falls in shock. "You've spoken with her?"

"For a few minutes." Rachel leans in with a wink and smiles. "Don't worry. I didn't tell her anything."

"What *did* you tell her?" Mrs. Smith demands.

"I told her we were just friends. I didn't tell her about the last time I saw

Brian and the last time I didn't see Brian." Rachel cocks her head with a sly smile.

Mrs. Smith drops her bags in a huff and reaches for Rachel's arm. Rachel yanks her arm away with more strength than she intended.

"Don't you dare think you can just grab me, Mrs. Smith," Rachel warns.

Mrs. Smith eyes Rachel warily and takes a step back. She breathes deeply before she continues.

"Listen, Rachel, don't do what I think you are going to do. You will destroy everything for him. Look at him. He's happy and he's much better off without you," Mrs. Smith says.

"What makes you think that?" Rachel folds her arms across her chest. Mrs. Smith may be right, but Rachel is not going to give in.

"Time has passed, Rachel. He's moved on ... and so should you," Mrs. Smith responds in a steely voice.

"I *have* moved on, Mrs. Smith. For your information, I have my own life. It's been ten years since I've seen him and he hasn't heard a peep from me in all that time," Rachel says.

"Then why are you here?" .

"I need to ask him something." Rachel turns in Brian's direction.

"You need to ask him something?"

"Yes."

"After all these years, and all this time, you decide to wait until the day before his wedding day to ask him something ..."

"Um, I didn't exactly wait—"

"Are you out of your mind? Whatever you have to say to Brian can wait until after the wedding."

"Well, actually, this doesn't concern you at all, Mrs. Smith. This is between me and Brian." Rachel straightens up and looks right into her eyes.

"You're acting like a child, Rachel. Do you think I'm going to let you ruin his wedding?"

"I'm not here to ruin any wedding. I just need to talk to Brian."

"You will do no such thing," Mrs. Smith says flippantly.

"Well, we'll see about that." Rachel walks around Mrs. Smith as she heads toward the ballroom.

Mrs. Smith grabs her arm again, but Rachel is too strong for her. They struggle in the middle of the foyer, but Rachel finally breaks from her grasp and makes her way inside the ballroom. She can see Brian at the end of the center aisle of the ballroom. Mrs. Smith enters the ballroom behind her and whispers to Rachel under her breath.

"Please, Rachel. Don't do this," she begs.

"I'm not doing anything. I just need to talk to him," she replies quietly and firmly and keeps walking. Mrs. Smith reaches back for her bags and follows on her heels.

All of the commotion at the entrance of the ballroom has finally gotten the attention of everyone in the room, especially Brian. After a few seconds, Brian recognizes the person coming his way.

"Rachel?" Brian quietly says to himself.

Rachel picks up the pace and lands right in front of Brian. "Brian," Rachel says with a broad smile as Mrs. Smith quickly rushes to stand next to her. Linda sidles alongside Brian.

"Brian, honey, look who's here for your rehearsal!" Linda says. Brian and Rachel stand right in front of each other without saying a word.

Rachel had a whole script written in her head, waiting for this exact moment to tell Brian what she had held deep inside. She would stay up nights thinking of how she would say it, or wondering if she would just let the moment dictate what needed to be said. She waited so long for this moment, but now she has nothing to say. *This isn't the right time*, Rachel thinks.

"Rachel, wha- what are you doing here?" Brian stammers, trying to work up a smile as he breaks the awkward silence between them.

"Well, Brian, I was in town visiting my mom and I ran into your mother this morning. She told me all about your wedding rehearsal. I told her that I wasn't going to be in town very long but she absolutely *insisted* that I come downtown just to say hi and wish you good luck," Rachel smiles brightly.

"I see." Brian glances over at his mother. "Well, that was very nice of Mother to invite you to the rehearsal."

"Well, it's the least I can do. You know, considering …"

"Considering what?" Linda kindly asks.

"Considering we've been friends for so long. I mean, how long has it been since we've seen each other?" Rachel asks.

"Uh, maybe a few years?" Brian answers.

"Ten years or something like that," Rachel replies as her smile fades away. Brian nods his head as he shifts his weight from one foot to another.

"It's funny how you two never kept in touch over the years," Linda says.

"I know! It is funny," Rachel says with an innocent smile as she watches Brian squirm while trying to keep his composure. She takes great pleasure in watching Mrs. Smith going through the same agony as well. Rachel never had an opportunity to really give it to Brian and Mrs. Smith. Now she is in the position to make him sweat off his GQ look, but Rachel isn't the vengeful type. She has other intentions for being here.

From the sound of blissful chatter coming from the foyer of the ballroom, it appears that Brian and Linda's wedding planner has finally arrived with two assistants in tow. The tall woman breezes in wearing a snow-covered coat and greets everyone closest to the entrance of the ballroom. Linda lights up when she sees her wedding coordinator.

"Oh my gosh, Brian. Crystal is here. Mrs. Smith, I want you to meet her if you have a sec?" Linda says excitedly.

"Well, I don't think—" Linda grabs Mrs. Smith's hand and drags her way from Brian and Rachel.

Rachel and Brian stand alone, facing each other for the first time in over ten years.

"You look very nice, Brian," Rachel says with a polite smile.

He doesn't know what is coming next, but has to respond. "Thank you, Rach." Rachel's mom never liked the nickname Brian gave her when they were kids, but Rachel saw it as a term of endearment.

"You're welcome." Rachel nods her head slightly.

Brian wants to end the conversation and get rid of her so he turns his head to find his mom.

"It looks like your mom is a little busy right now." He looks over to find his mom embroiled in some animated conversation with the wedding planner. Rachel is right. He's stuck with her for at least the next couple of minutes.

Brian forces a smile. "I remember when you used to wear that coat all the time. As a matter of fact, when I saw you I thought we went back in time or something. The green sweatshirt, and those jeans—"

"I didn't have anything else to wear, Brian. My clothes got left behind," she interjects and looks directly into his eyes. Her arms are folded across her chest and she stands as still as a statue. Nothing in her body language gives him any indication if he is making the situation better or worse.

"Left behind?" Brian raises his eyebrows in surprise.

"In Seattle," Rachel says with an icy tone.

"Oh. That's odd."

"Huh, you think that's odd?" Rachel asks in a challenging voice.

Brian steps back when he hears that tone in her voice. He looks over his shoulder again, but his mother is nowhere to be seen. "Rach, what are you doing here?" She doesn't react but continues to stare at him. "Rach?"

"You're not even going to ask me how I am?" Rachel finally asks.

"Okay then. How are you?" Beads of sweat roll down his brow.

"I've been better," Rachel says.

"Great. Now what are you doing here?" Brian growls. He knows she won't like that tone, but he needs this problem to go away.

"Not even an apology, huh?" Rachel says.

"Is that why you're here, Rach? You came all this way for me to apologize to you?"

"Were you *ever* going to apologize to me, Brian? Ever?"

"Didn't you read the letter?" Brian asks.

She smiles, leans over to Brian, and speaks to him in a soft voice. "Brian, sweetie, did you think a fucking letter was going to make everything you did to me okay? Did you think I was going to say 'oh, poor Brian' when you stood me up on our wedding day? Did you think a letter would make everything all right again? Tell me, Brian, is that what you thought?" Rachel asks firmly with a smile.

Rachel has *never* spoken to Brian in that manner before. Brian's worst nightmare is slowly unfolding before his eyes. The woman that he left at the altar over ten years ago now stands before him at his own wedding rehearsal with a different woman altogether. He has never told Linda about what happened, and Rachel knows it. She is in the position to completely ruin his wedding and there is nothing he can do about it. He will not be able to walk away from this.

CHAPTER
FIVE

I'm waiting in the Lounge Room at the church with Mom. Her constant pacing is making me freak out inside. I stand like a statue, waiting to get this show started, but fucking Brian is late. I can hear my mom talking to herself, getting angrier by the minute. My mom is usually the super chill one, and to tell the truth I don't think I have ever seen her this angry. I'm afraid to walk over and try to calm her down. It's best that I say nothing right now.

My mom never took me to church or a synagogue, so I'm not really the praying type, but for every second I look out that window and DON'T see Brian, I make one prayer to Jesus, Moses, and whomever else can hear me. Brian is fifteen minutes late. All I see is that stupid white limo parked in front, waiting for the ceremony to end. He had better be in an accident or held up for some other reason.

Then I hear a quiet knock on the door. It's Mrs. Brown, one of the church's administrators. She peeks her head into the room slowly as she pushes the creaky door open.

"Any word, sweetie?" she politely asks. My mom doesn't say anything. She just keeps pacing and mumbling to herself.

"No, Mrs. Brown," I say without turning around to face her.

"Honey, I just spoke with Father Dolan a moment ago. He said that he'll give it another fifteen minutes. After that, he will have to call it off for today," Mrs. Brown says softly with a note of sadness in her voice. I can hear my mom's pacing getting louder and louder. I keep my eyes peeled to the window for any sign of Brian.

"Thank you, Mrs. Brown. We understand. Tell Father Dolan we appreciate his patience."

Mrs. Brown leaves the room, closing the door gently behind her.

"That asshole," my mom whispers to herself. "That fucking asshole."

"Mom, you're not making this situation any easier."

All of a sudden, my mom stops pacing. "What's wrong with that boy?! I'm going to wring his neck as soon as I see him."

I just keep looking out of the window with sweat pouring down my body in that big puffy dress. My head swims in utter devastation, and I clutch my hands together because I have nothing else to hold on to. He's stood me up before, but I never thought he would be capable of doing this.

Just when I think all hope is lost, a white Cadillac pulls up in front of the church. With a sharp intake of breath, I lean on to the windowsill and hope to see Brian getting out of that car. Please, God, let it be Brian. I let my mom ramble on about him until I know for sure that it's him. The passenger door opens and my heart beats uncontrollably. Mrs. Smith steps out of the car wearing an off-white dress. She closes the car door, but where is Brian? Mrs. Smith walks up the front steps and enters the church with no Brian in sight. Oh fuck. This isn't good.

"Did I hear a car pull up?" my mom suddenly asks and heads over to the window. I don't say anything. I don't know what to do. I just keep staring out the window hoping Brian jumps out of that car any minute. Mom peers at the parked Cadillac through the window. "Is that Brian?"

Then we hear a soft knock at the door. I know exactly who it is. I don't want to walk over to the door to open it. Then the door slowly opens. I turn around to see Mrs. Smith. She enters the room with a large envelope in her hand. Oh crap.

"Hello Sylvia—" Mrs. Smith says.

"Maureen, where the hell is Brian?" my mom bellows and stops Mrs. Smith in her tracks. I can tell from Mrs. Smith's stiff posture that she is the bearer of bad news. She exhales and slowly turns towards me.

"I'm really sorry, Rachel. He's not coming." Mrs. Smith shakes her head.

My mom immediately jumps in front of Mrs. Smith to protect me from this horrible blow. "Brian's not coming?! He can't do that, Maureen! We have a church full of people who have traveled thousands of miles to see Rachel get married. There's no way in hell he's going to do that to my baby!" my mom screams at Mrs. Smith. In spite of everything, it's good to see my tiny mom defend me against a woman who stands close to six feet tall.

I can't say anything. I am in utter shock that this is actually happening. My mom looks like she is about to go to blows with Mrs. Smith, her best friend. I need to jump in to keep them from fighting.

"Mom?" I ask softly. "Let me talk to Mrs. Smith."

"No, Rachel," my mom snaps back as she stares at Maureen. "Anything you need to say to my daughter, you say to me too."

"Mom! Please!" I yell. Oh my God. I can't believe I just said that to my mom. I have never, ever raised my voice to my mom like that. She turns to me in utter surprise. Even though I want to yell at Mrs. Smith, I have to be the peacemaker right now. I need to know where he is. I might still be able to make this work. I know I can. "Mom, you don't need to fight my battles for me anymore. I'm a big girl now. Please, give us a minute. I'll call you if I need you." It takes every bit of courage and strength to say that to her. I reach out to hold her shaking hand and manage to calm her down.

"Alright. I'll be right outside if you need me," Mom says. She slowly lets go of my hand, walks out of the room, and closes the door behind her.

As soon as the door closes, Mrs. Smith walks over and hands me the sealed envelope. I don't even look at her as I hold the envelope down in front of me. Brian didn't even bother to put my name on the envelope. What a jerk.

"Where's Brian, Mrs. Smith?" I ask.

"I can't tell you," Mrs. Smith says.

"Where is he?" I ask again.

"Rachel—"

"Where the hell is he?!" I interrupt forcefully. Mrs. Smith pauses a moment and takes a breath.

"Everything is in the letter, Rachel. Brian wanted to tell you himself—"

"No he didn't. He could have been a man and told me to my face. Instead, he sends his mommy," I smirk. "You always do the dirty work for him, don't you."

"Rachel. Listen—"

I cut her off again and get right in her face. "What the fuck is the matter with him?! I don't get it! Really, I just don't get it! This isn't about someone having cold feet. All of these years we've known each other. We grew up together. We've done so much together. I've always been there whenever he needed me. All these years and now he does this to me. I never thought in a million years he would ever do this to me. Never."

I finally understand what has happened. Brian has left me here to fend for myself amongst the sharks. I will have to deal with the sad faces and judgmental glances when everyone in that church finds out that he stood me up at the altar. I'm too hurt to say anything more. I feel my heart utterly deflate and can't look at her anymore. This is it. It's over.

The room goes quiet for a minute. I step away from Mrs. Smith. Silence fills the room.

"You know as well as I do that he's left you waiting for him before, Rachel," Mrs. Smith says in a patronizing tone.

"But not at his own wedding, Mrs. Smith," I shoot back and get right in her face. "We planned every part of this wedding together: the invitations, the ceremony, the rehearsal dinner, the wedding brunch the next day, and not one word. Not one fucking word."

"Well, you can be a little difficult to talk to sometimes. He wanted to postpone the wedding and you knew that," Mrs. Smith replies.

"He never mentioned anything to me about postponing it," I say.

"Rachel, we buried his father just three months ago. Three months ago. Don't you think he needed more time to grieve?" She takes a step closer to me and softens her voice. "You knew deep down that you were both rushing into this. He wasn't ready. Can't you get that through your head, Rachel?"

"Oh, now the both of you are going to use Ted's death as an excuse for this too. Don't you think it's a little old to keep blaming his dead father whenever you two do something wrong?"

Without an ounce of hesitation, Mrs. Smith raises her hand and SLAPS me in the face.

I saw the hand coming, but I couldn't believe that she would strike me. It seemed liked it all happened in slow motion, but I did nothing to stop it. I stumble back from the impact, holding my hand over my face. Mrs. Smith just slapped me. On my wedding day. I keep my distance. I don't know if I should strike back or not. I don't know. All I can do is stand there in shock.

All of a sudden I see tears rushing down Mrs. Smith's face, frozen like an old Roman statue. Her eyes look right through me as her mascara runs slightly down the side of her beet-red cheeks. I've never seen this woman cry before. Not even at Ted's funeral. I always thought she was a cold, distant person, but here she stands weeping in front of me.

"You've never, ever considered his feelings, Rachel," Mrs. Smith blurts through her tears. "The wedding was your idea. His decision to quit college, his decision to leave his band, and just about everything he has done in the last fifteen years were all your ideas. You have never given him an ounce of space to live his own life. When he was trying date other girls, you always had to get in the way. You even wanted to control how he grieved his father's death. Rachel, he loved his father very much. His death hurt him more than you know. You say you care for him, yet you never even bothered to ask him how he feels. I wish you would have stopped being so damn selfish and maybe listened to him for once in your life."

The room gets quiet for a split second. My mom bursts through the door and sees us facing each other in our post-fighting stance, emotionally licking our wounds. She looks at the both of us with my hand over my face and mascara running down Mrs. Smith's face.

"*What just happened?*" *my mother demands. My body leans over from sheer exhaustion but my eyes stay locked on Mrs. Smith. None of this was supposed to happen. Anything I try to do or say right now will only make the situation worse. The wedding is off and there is nothing I can do about it. I can't fix it. I won't run off looking for him to try and make it all better. I'm not going to do anything. I just want to go home.*

"*You can leave now, Mrs. Smith,*" *I say. I can't believe she treated me this way. When we were little she was such a sweet, caring person, especially around Brian. She would laugh and smile whenever they played together in the backyard. But the train accident changed all of that.*

When Brian was eight, he and his mother set out on an express train that derailed because the operator drove the train too fast for the tracks to handle. They were in the first car when it ran off the tracks and hit the side of an apartment complex. Only a handful of people survived the crash when the first set of cars hit the building. Brian was so injured that they thought he wasn't going to make it. He and Mrs. Smith eventually recovered but they became cold and distant in their own way.

The look that Mrs. Smith gives me now is the same look she had when she thought Brian was going to die from his injuries. What a horrible memory.

"*You'd better leave now, Maureen,*" *my mom finally jumps in. Mrs. Smith takes a step back from me, looks at my mother for a moment, and then finally walks out of the room.*

Mom waits until the door closes before she says anything. "What just happened?"

"*Mom, you can tell everyone that there isn't going to be a wedding. Brian is not coming,*" *I say. I think she already knew that.*

"*What did Maureen say to you?*"

"*Nothing I didn't already know,*" *I say. "You were right. You knew he wasn't coming. You were right all along."*

I walk over to the couch in the room and sink down into the cushions in my big dress. What a horrible day. With nothing else to say, I simply look out of the window.

"They did say it was going to rain today anyway," I say. "Who gets married on a day it's supposed to rain. You know I don't like it when it rains, Mom. It gets me all congested."

"That's true …," Mom says. I don't look over at my mom. I wasn't even sure I wanted her to do anything to make me feel better. I'm just too embarrassed to do anything but look down at my very beautiful white shoes.

"Mom, I don't think I can go out there. I—"

"Don't worry about it, dear. I'll get rid of everyone. You don't have to do anything. Just wait for me, okay? Promise me, Rachel, that you're not going to go anywhere."

She thinks I'm going to run off to find him. That would have been a good guess on her part. She knows me pretty well. I've done it before.

Not this time. Not anymore.

"I'm not going anywhere, Mom. Where else would I go? I just want to be left alone for a little bit."

"Sure." My mom walks out of the room and closes the door behind her.

I get up and walk over to the window. I don't see it, but I can hear the rain falling down. This wasn't the best day to get married, anyway. All I have is this stupid letter Brian wrote me.

I'll read it later.

BRIAN AND Rachel stand right in front of each other as the rest of the wedding party prepares for the rehearsal. Brian runs through different options in his mind that might diffuse the situation. He isn't sure what else to do now. He decides to *finally* have the discussion with Rachel that he dreaded all these years.

"Rachel, I couldn't marry you. I couldn't marry anyone. You just didn't understand," Brian said, trying to keep the argument into a whisper.

"I could have made time to understand if you had been man enough to tell me. You could have done it … I don't know … *ANY TIME* before our wedding day! You humiliated me, Brian. You embarrassed me in front of my mom and my whole family. What did I ever do to deserve that?" Rachel hisses.

The fact that Rachel hasn't started screaming gives Brian some small measure of comfort. Maybe she just needs to tell him her feelings about the whole situation. Brian thinks if he can just let her do what she wants, then maybe this will all end quietly and he can convince her to leave.

"Alright. I'm sorry, Rachel. I'm very sorry that I left you standing there by yourself. I should have told you I had second thoughts about the wedding. I never intended to hurt you, but you're right. Leaving you there with only a letter to explain my actions was not the smartest idea. As a matter of fact, it ended up being a very dumb idea. Please believe me it had nothing to do with you. I am truly, truly sorry, Rachel," he whispers with regret.

Rachel leans back and looks him right in the eye with an impish smile. "See, Brian. That wasn't so hard, was it?"

Her sudden politeness takes Brian by surprise. He expected so much worse. Once when they were young she lost her temper and became uncontrollably violent toward him. Maybe that was the reason he had never confronted her about not going through with the wedding. He was afraid of her reaction if he did try to call it off. Now he's afraid of what she will do next.

"You forgive me?" Brian asks warily.

"Yes, Brian, I forgive you. You did an absolutely awful thing to me. Actually, you have done a lot of awful things to me over the years. I could just stand here and rehash old memories, but why dwell on the past. Life goes on, right?" Rachel shrugs her shoulders and offers a light smile to her former friend.

"Yeah, you could say that," Brian says.

"Good. I'm glad we got that out of the way."

"So am I. All is forgiven?"

"All is forgiven. Not forgotten, though," Rachel warns.

Brian breathes a sigh of relief. He might be able to resolve this situation sooner than he thought. "Wow, Rachel. As soon as I saw you, I thought you were going to do something crazy—"

"Like ruin your wedding day?" Rachel interrupts.

"No. You know what I mean."

"Don't worry. I'm not a jerk like you, Brian." She immediately doesn't like the way the words come out. "I'm sorry. I didn't mean to say that. I just want to keep the peace."

Brian looks up sheepishly. "Well, you do have a right to say it."

"I have a right to say anything I want to you, don't I?" Rachel asks.

"Yeah. You do," Brian says. Now might be a good time to extend an olive branch. "You know, Rach, maybe after the wedding, when I get back, we can go out for lunch or something. We can catch up."

"Well, Brian, I don't live here anymore so that would be pretty hard to do. Besides, I had no intention of seeing you at all. I just found out today that you were getting married so I thought I'd come down and say my piece." She relaxes her shoulders and takes a breath. "But now that I'm here, I'd like to see if you could help me with something."

"Oh. Well, sure. What do you need me to do?" Brian asks, hoping the task is a simple one.

"I need you to do me a favor, Brian." Rachel says.

"A favor? Sure, Rach. I can do a favor for you. It's the least I can do."

Rachel nods but says nothing in response.

"Well, what is it?"

"That's the thing. I can't tell you."

"You can't tell me. Why can't you tell me?"

"I just can't," Rachel says.

"Then how can I help you, Rach, if I don't know what's going on? "

"You're just going to have to trust me, Brian."

"Alright, then. So at some point, you're going to tell me, right? When do I do this favor for you?"

"Tomorrow."

"Tomorrow? Tomorrow's my wedding."

"It shouldn't take long."

Brian shakes his head. "No, Rachel. I can't do it on my wedding day."

"Why not?"

"Because I'm getting married! You don't just ask someone to do a favor for you on their wedding day."

"You owe me, Brian," Rachel says quietly.

"I know I do, Rachel. I don't contest that, but on my wedding day? That's not fair."

"I know it's your special day, but I wouldn't be here asking for your help if it wasn't important."

"Rachel, nothing is that important."

"Well, this is …"

"Then tell me what is so important that you need me to do without telling me what it is … on my wedding day?"

"I just can't tell you, Brian."

"You can't tell me. If you can't tell me, then you know very well that I can't do it."

"What I know is that I have never asked you to do anything for me since that day you stood me up ten years ago. Nothing. You got away with humiliating me on my wedding day without even an angry word from me. Now, I am asking you to do one favor and you can't even do that."

"You're crazy, Rach. You always were."

"If our past meant anything to you at all, you will just do this for me," Rachel says.

"No. I don't know what you're up to, but I still wouldn't do it, especially on my wedding day. You need to get over me, Rach. There's nothing between us anymore."

Rachel reels back in disgust from that last comment and decides to back off.

"Alright then, Brian. I understand. It was wrong of me to ask you for a favor on your wedding day. It was also wrong of me to come down here and spoil your special occasion. I'm sorry, Brian."

Her apology leaves Brian dumbfounded since she rarely apologized for anything when they were young.

"Apology accepted," Brian stammers.

"Good." She smiles, finds a seat in one of the rehearsal chairs lined neatly in a row, and makes herself comfortable.

Seeing this, Brian trots over to where she is sitting and leans into her ear. "What are you doing?" he whispers.

"What?" Rachel whispers back.

"What do you mean, *what*? You're just going to sit here?"

"Yeah. I want to see the rehearsal. Since I came all the way down here, I might as well see how it's going to end."

"You can't stay."

"What?"

"You can't stay, Rach."

"Why not?"

"You know very well why not. This is *my* wedding rehearsal, Rach, and I never invited you. You need to go."

"No." Rachel turns toward the altar.

"What do you mean, no?"

"No, I'm staying for the rehearsal. Your fiancée invited me to stay, so I'm staying."

"Rach, don't make me throw you out," Brian warns.

"Ha! I'd like to see you try," Rachel sneers.

Brian reaches for her arm, and Rachel quickly leans into his ear and whispers, "Make no mistake, Brian. If you don't let me go right now, I will make a scene and tell everyone what you did at another wedding many years ago."

"You wouldn't." Brian pulls back in fear.

"Don't even try me, Brian. I would think you'd know me by now." Rachel smiles.

Brian looks over and sees more people entering the ballroom. He knows that Rachel has all the leverage right now. Even if he did confess his relationship with Rachel to Linda, he would never be able to explain standing her up at the altar. It appears that Brian will have to deal with Rachel for the duration of the evening. He can tell that she meant what she said. Whenever she had that look of determination, nothing would stand in her way. She always got her way when they were kids, and this time he gave her all the ammo that she needed to do whatever she wanted. After all, she was asked to stay for the rehearsal by Linda. What more could he do? He would just have to trust that she would refrain from doing anything to jeopardize his relationship with Linda. In the past he could only trust Rachel to be prompt or to help him when needed. Everything else was a crapshoot of broken promises with her fingers permanently crossed behind her back.

"Okay, Rachel. You win. You can stay," Brian spits out through pursed lips.

"I can stay?" Rachel exclaims with forced exuberance. "Great!"

"Promise me you're not going to do anything to embarrass me. Okay?"

"Me? Definitely not." She shakes her head with wide, innocent eyes.

"You promise?"

"I promise."

"You promise. That was too easy. You're not crossing your fingers, are you?" Brian says.

"Brian, that's so second grade."

"Just checking. Look, after the rehearsal maybe we can chat a little. We can talk about this favor thing. Alright?"

"Sure, Brian."

He looks down at her hands to see if any of her fingers were crossed. It's a childish reaction, but with Rachel he was never sure.

"Okay. I will see you afterwards?" Brian asks.

"Sure." Brian walks away to greet the new set of people attending the rehearsal. Rachel settles into her chair and waits for the show to begin.

Mrs. Smith comes over and slides into a chair in front of Rachel. She quickly turns around to face her. "You need to leave, Rachel."

Rachel rolls her eyes and looks away from Mrs. Smith. "Brian said I could stay."

"What? No, he didn't."

"He did. You can ask him right now."

Mrs. Smith leans over to Rachel in a supplicant manner. "Rachel. Please don't do what I think you're going to do."

"And what would that be?"

"After all these years, you don't think I know you by now?" Mrs. Smith asks.

Rachel snorts and shakes her head. "I gave him my word that I would not do anything to embarrass him."

"Rachel, I wish I could believe you, I really do, but you've always intruded upon affairs that don't concern you."

"This does concern me, you know. After all, he was supposed to get married to me," Rachel snaps.

"Rachel, please. That's all over now."

"Oh, I know."

"Then for the love of God, why are you staying?"

"If you must know, I asked him if he would do me a favor," Rachel huffs.

"A favor?" Mrs. Smith asks.

"Yep. I asked him if he could help me do something."

"And?"

"Well, he said he couldn't, considering tomorrow is his wedding day," Rachel says.

Mrs. Smith throws her hands up in shock. "Rachel! Are you crazy? You asked him to do some silly favor on his wedding day?"

"It isn't a silly favor," Rachel says.

"Then tell me what it is," Mrs. Smith demands.

"I can't tell you."

"You can't tell me." She shakes her head. "You're being ridiculous."

Rachel sighs. "Look, I just went over this with Brian. I don't feel like going through this again with you too."

"Do you even know what you're saying?"

Just as the conversation is about to get very heated, Brian and Linda, along with some members of the wedding party, approach them.

"Hey, Rachel, I booked a private dining room across the street from the hotel for the rehearsal dinner. We're all heading there after this is done. I would love it if you had time to come down and hang out with us for a bit," Linda says.

Sensing the attention of the entire room now focused on her, Rachel stands up to chat with Linda more directly.

"I know you have to catch a flight out tonight, but would you have time to stay for a drink or two," entreats Linda.

"Oh wow. I don't know. I don't want to intrude." Rachel glances over at Brian and Mrs. Smith with a seemingly genuine look of concern.

"No, no. Don't give it a second thought. Please, we would love to have you. Besides, I would love it if you would tell us more stories about Brian when he was a kid. Brian is very closed off about his past," Linda says.

"He's always been like that. Right, Brian?" Rachel smiles and watches him panic on the inside, wondering if their secret will come out. Rachel seems to enjoy putting Brian on the spot, especially in front of his mom.

"Right, Rach," Brian finally responds.

Rachel turns back to Linda. "We met in preschool, then we carried on as friends throughout grammar school and high school. We were in many of the same classes. From there, we graduated and parted ways."

"Really?" Linda asks. "Why?"

"Well, that's a good question. Brian?" Rachel punts the question to Brian.

"I guess we just grew up and moved on," Brian responds.

"Grew up and moved on," Rachel repeats. She pauses for a few seconds. "Yeah, that's the best way to put it."

"Rachel, didn't you say you two were best friends?" Linda asks.

"Oh yeah. We did everything together when we were kids," Rachel says.

"Oh wow. What's the one thing you remember about Brian the most?" Linda asks.

"Huh ... that's a good one. Wow, there were so many. I don't think there was ever just one thing," Rachel says with a laugh.

"Isn't there anything that comes to mind right now?" Linda asks.

Rachel takes a moment to come up with a story. "Okay, we were kids ... I'd say about nine or so. He had this thing about running away from me. As soon as he saw me walking towards him, he would let out this scream and would just run off. I would try to chase him, but he was always the faster one and I could never catch up. Well, one day he did the thing he would always do, scream and run off at the first sight of me. I decided that I would do whatever I could to catch him. I dropped my things and ran as fast as I could to chase him. And this lasted for a few good minutes. Eventually, he ran off toward a small lake near our house. I didn't see where he went, but I knew he was nearby. I ran up to this small pier by the lake to see where he went. For some reason I looked down and there he was ... in the water."

Everyone was captivated by the story, especially Linda. "Then what happened?" she asks.

"Well, I ran down to the end of the pier and grabbed a long rope that was coiled up on the dock. I tied one end to a rail, the other around my waist, and jumped in after Brian. I got him and pulled him to the side of the dock. As soon as I yanked him out of the water, he screamed and ran off again, like nothing happened." Rachel chuckles.

"Was he drowning?" Linda asks.

"Oh no. He just thought he had found the perfect hiding place from me. I wrapped the rope around me because I didn't know how to swim, but it turns out he was in the shallow part of the water. He was fine. He was just embarrassed that I caught him again, as usual," Rachel says. Everyone laughs about the funny story, except Brian and Mrs. Smith.

Brian and Rachel both know there is a lot more to that story than what she told everyone. All Mrs. Smith remembers was that Brian came home crying, all wet in the middle of winter, and he never told her what had happened to him. Usually Rachel was always nearby when something strange happened to

Brian, but she was nowhere to be found. Mrs. Smith kept asking him what had happened, but he never revealed the truth. After a few days, she simply stopped asking about it and for some odd reason, Rachel stopped coming by the house for at least a couple of weeks. Mrs. Smith knew something had occurred between the two of them, but since he was okay, she didn't think much of it.

"So, where did you two meet?" Rachel said to Linda, trying to keep the lively conversation going.

"Well, I'm a Meeting Concierge for the Rochester Hotel down the street. We work together, of course," Linda says.

"Work together?" Rachel asks.

"You know he's the Director of AV for the hotel, right?" Linda says.

"Director of AV for the hotel. Oh *sure*. Of course," Rachel says with a shrug, playing it off as though she knew what he did for a living.

"You didn't know he was working for the hotel?" Linda asks.

"Oh no. I'd heard he worked for the hotel. I just didn't know he got promoted to *Director* of AV. Congratulations, Brian." She can see Brian getting slightly angry.

"The hotel loves him. Everyone loves him. He's great with clients, and he's so technical," Linda says.

"Well, you probably didn't know that we used to worked together in the AV department in grammar school," Rachel says cheerfully.

"Really?" Linda lights up. "He never mentioned anything to me about that."

"Oh yeah, that's how he got started. He joined the AV department, and then I followed right behind him. We were a great team," Rachel says. "We were both a couple of nerdy kids back then. Now he's so much cooler."

"That's right," Linda says as she grabs his arms and pulls him towards her in a show of pride and affection. Some commotion is heard from the back of the room. Other members of Linda's family have arrived.

"Sorry guys, I would love to hear more, but I need to greet the others. I will be right back," Linda says. She kisses Brian on the cheek and runs off with the rest of the rehearsal party. Now Rachel is alone with Brian and his mother.

"Director of AV, huh," Rachel says. "I knew so much more about AV than you did."

"Rachel, I know this is so much fun for you, but you can obviously see how important this is to Brian," Mrs. Smith says. "Why don't you just leave right now? We can make some excuse for you."

"I'm trying to remember the last time I saw the both of you together. Wait, it was when we were at the Freeman Club. We were making our last deposit for the reception place," Rachel says.

"Rach—" Brian interrupts.

"Wait, Brian. I'm not finished," Rachel quickly replies. "We were walking around the ballroom. The mirrors, the dance floor, the entrance to the place, you hated everything about it. I didn't say anything. I just thought it was nerves, but your mom was no help at all." Then Rachel directs herself to his mom. "And you just kept telling him to postpone it. 'Postpone it, sweetie. She will understand,' is all I heard you whisper to him. You're not whispering that to him right now, are you?"

"Rach, is this what you came down here for … to make me miserable?" Brian asks.

"That was not my intention, Brian. Though I am getting some satisfaction in watching you squirm."

"Rachel!" his mother exclaims.

"Brian, are you going to do that favor for me or what?" Rachel interjects.

"Rachel, I'm not going to do it. Not on my wedding day. No matter what you say or do. I will not drop everything to come help you do something, and you won't even tell me what it is," Brian says.

"But you owe me," Rachel says.

"He owes you nothing, Rachel," his mother hisses.

"He owes me for more than you will ever admit. Isn't that right, Brian?"

"Rachel. I'm with Linda now," Brian says, as if talking to a child.

"Yes, I can see that. She's a great girl, Brian. I like her a lot."

"We are over," he says, gesturing between himself and Rachel. "You can see that as well, right?"

"I do see that. Thank you for pointing out the obvious." Rachel rolls her eyes.

"There really isn't a favor you need from me, is there?" Brian asks.

"Do you really think I made all of this up just to screw things up with you and Linda? I couldn't care less about who you marry. That part of my life is over. I just need your help, Brian."

Rachel starts to feel dizzy. Brian and his mother notice Rachel swaying from side to side, but say nothing. She slowly gets up from her chair and walks off. She focuses on walking out of the ballroom without passing out. Her quick departure goes unnoticed by everyone … everyone except Linda.

She makes it out of the ballroom and into the foyer. Rachel sees the ladies' bathroom around the corner and quickly heads over. Once in the bathroom she finds an open stall. She enters, closes the stall door behind her, and then throws up. Dropping to her knees, Rachel begins to drift in and out of consciousness. She's holding on to the toilet as she tries not to fall completely on the floor. As her regurgitation ends, she finds her footing and slowly stands up. Rachel reaches her hand through her hair and finds it wet with blood. Her wound opened up … again. She applies toilet paper to it as she slouches over the toilet.

"Rachel, are you okay?" Rachel hears a gentle voice coming from the entrance of the bathroom. Linda. Rachel straightens up but stays in the stall. She hears her walk up to the stall door. "Are you okay?" Linda asks again.

"Yeah …" Rachel replies in a shaky voice. She clears her throat to steady her voice. "I just wasn't feeling well for a second there. Jet lag, maybe."

"I see." Linda faces the stall door. "Sorry if I'm intruding, but I noticed that the conversation between you, Brian, and his mom didn't seem very cordial. Is there something wrong?"

"Tell me something, Linda. Do you like Mrs. Smith?" Rachel dabs away the blood on her forehead with toilet tissue.

"Mrs. Smith? I think she's the sweetest lady. She's been nothing but nice to me," Linda says.

"Wow, that's good. Mrs. Smith and I used to be very close when I was little. After all, she was my mother's best friend for a time."

"And are they still friends?" Linda asks.

"Well, not really. They kind of grew apart, like Brian and me."

Linda hesitates for a moment. "Is that what really happened between the two of you?"

Rachel stops patting her forehead and looks up at the stall door in shock. "The two of us?"

"Between you and Brian. I mean, I think it's kind of strange that after all this time I've known him he's never mentioned you at all. It seems to me that you two meant a lot more to each other than what the both of you are saying."

Linda is apparently more perceptive than Rachel first thought, and she has to respect that. Rachel needs to decide. She can just tell Linda the truth or play along hoping that Brian will change his mind about doing the favor.

"Funny you should say that. You're very observant," Rachel says.

"Well, I am marrying him tomorrow. Should I be concerned?"

"About Brian?"

"No, about you."

Should Linda be concerned about me? Maybe ten years ago, but not anymore.

Rachel's head starts throbbing in pain. As she struggles to remain upright, she makes a decision to paint Brian in the best light just so that Linda would leave the bathroom.

"I can tell you with the utmost certainty that you definitely don't have to worry about me. We were close, but understand we only lived a block away from each other. For about sixteen years, we did just about everything together. We were more like brother and sister than friends. Our parents never had any more kids, so we just had each other. We took care of each other," Rachel says with a smile. "You know what the funny thing is about us? We're polar opposites in the worst way. Well, that's not true. We were both terribly unpopular at school. We were very different compared to the other kids and got picked on a lot. But you know, he always looked out for me and I did the same for him. I guess that's why we were such good friends for so long," Rachel explains.

Rachel never had to summarize their relationship like that before. There was so much more to it than that, but she needs Linda to believe that they were just friends. She has the power to destroy Brian's life right now, but she would never do that to him.

"Just friends?" Linda asks quietly.

"Just friends."

"Good friends don't just move on and stop seeing each other over ten years." There's got to be something more to it than that. It sounds like you two had a special connection, and then you just stop talking? I don't buy it," she says. *Damn, this girl is definitely smarter than I expected.*

"Yeah, you're right. There was something else, " Rachel confesses. Linda waits for her to elaborate and says nothing for a moment.

"Well? What else?" Linda asks.

"He thinks I killed his father," Rachel says.

"What?"

"He thinks I killed his father," Rachel sighs.

"Killed his father? I don't understand."

Rachel can't stand anymore. She leans down to sit on the toilet while still applying pressure to her wound.

"My car got stuck in a bad blizzard the year we graduated from high school. I was nineteen at the time. His father, one of the greatest human beings to walk this planet, was kind enough to help me dig out my car so I could go to work that night. It was very slushy snow. Very heavy. I told him he didn't have to help me, but he did anyway. Soon after he started shoveling, he suffered a heart attack and died right there in front of me," Rachel says. "I tried to revive him, but … he just died. I called for an ambulance, but it was too late. The storm slowed down everything," Rachel pauses for a second. "And for some strange reason, Brian blamed me for his death. So did his mom. Things were never the same between us after that."

"Brian never mentioned that to me before," Linda says softly.

"He *did* mention that he died, right?"

"He did, but he never mentioned *that* part of the story."

"Didn't he tell you how he died?" Rachel asks.

"He was shoveling snow out in front of the house and had a heart attack," Linda says.

"I don't blame him for changing the story one bit."

"Why wouldn't he tell me the truth about how his father died?"

"It's a little bit more complicated than that."

"What was so complicated?"

"His father had a heart condition and even though he offered to help, I didn't do anything to stop him. Brian and his mom always blamed me for allowing him to help in spite of his condition. I don't know. Maybe it was my fault. My own dad skipped out on me before I was born, so Ted was the only father figure I've ever had. I loved it whenever he went out of his way to help me. He was such a wonderful, caring person and always found a way to make me a part of his family so I wouldn't feel so lonely. It was like he had a daughter, he would tell me from time to time. Brian never understood that." Rachel looks away from the door and slumps against the toilet seat. It made her sad to think about Ted. She didn't want to relive that night, but she needed Linda to understand why things got so bad between her and Brian.

"I'm sorry that happened to you, Rachel."

"Thank you."

"Was there anything else I should know about?" Linda asks.

"Anything else?"

"I mean, this is kind of a big deal. Why wouldn't he ever mention what really happened when his father died? That was such a traumatic thing for him and it makes me wonder what else he's keeping from me."

Rachel couldn't stay in the stall anymore. She needed to look Linda in the eyes and straighten everything out. Linda steps back to let Rachel come out but notices the bloody tissue she holds against her forehead.

"Oh my God, Rachel, are you okay? You're bleeding!"

"Yeah. I got into an accident recently. I bumped my head in the stall and reopened the wound. It's not that big of a deal." Rachel leans up against the wall next to the stall, facing Linda. "His father's passing was a big deal," Rachel continues. "It was a very big deal for Brian and he took it harder than anyone. He adored his father very much. My mother and I loved each other, but it was nothing like the connection Brian had with his father. He must have showed you the countless pictures and videos his dad used to take of him. Ted was probably the greatest friend he had ever had. His death killed our relationship," Rachel says.

"Relationship?" Linda's head jerks up.

"What?" Rachel looks up to Linda as if in a daze.

"You said relationship." Linda narrows her eyes.

I slipped, Rachel thinks. *I wasn't supposed to say that.* Did Linda trick Rachel into saying something she didn't mean to say?

"Relationship? Sorry, I meant to say friendship." Rachel quickly shakes her head.

"You two *did* have something together, didn't you?" Linda accuses.

"Linda, please. It's not what you think."

"Oh my God! I'm marrying that man tomorrow and I don't even know who he is!" Linda starts pacing the bathroom, and hyperventilating, looking as if she might pass out. Rachel realizes that the situation is quickly deteriorating. She rushes to Linda and grabs both arms.

"Listen, it's not what you think. You have to believe me."

Linda yanks her arms out of Rachel's hands. "Believe you? I just met you!"

"I know, I know, but please hear me out. Please?" Rachel looks directly into Linda's eyes as she finally calms down. "When two people have gone through as much as we have throughout the years, they develop a special relationship.

We went through a lot of things together, good and bad. I carry that connection with him always, regardless of what he becomes or whom he marries. We parted ways. We grew apart. That happens." Rachel exhales deeply and shakes her head. "You know, he doesn't even know I'm married!"

"What?" Linda says in surprise as she backs away from her.

Rachel leans against the wall. "Yeah. That's how bad our friendship is now. The biggest moment in my life, and I never even bothered to share that part of my life with him."

"Why?" Linda asks.

"We needed to live our own separate lives after being around each other for so long. Look at him now. I've never seen him this happy before. He's such a different person than when I last saw him. He got rid of his dorky glasses and that ugly beard and moustache and looks like he's even been working out. He's not the same guy he was several years ago. To tell you the truth, I almost didn't recognize him at first. Our separation changed him for the better," Rachel says.

"Really?" Linda relaxes her body, just a bit.

"Really. I mean, when he saw me with my coat and jeans on, he probably thought we went through some time warp. I'm wearing the same clothes I used to wear when I was a teenager. It probably brought back a lot of pain when he saw me today. I'm only wearing these clothes because the airline lost my luggage on the flight in and these were the only clothes my mom had available," Rachel says.

"Oh, I'm sorry," Linda says.

"That's all right." Rachel brightens up. "See? This isn't as big a deal as you think. I just came down to see him while I was in town, say hi, and that's it."

"That's it?" Linda asks.

"That's it," Rachel says firmly. She can finally see Linda's face melt with relief. "Do you feel better about everything now?"

"Well, I think I do. That was a lot to learn about my future husband the night before my wedding," Linda says. *She's right. It was a lot to take in*, Rachel thinks.

"I know. He's such a jerk for not saying anything, but, as usual, he's not one to reveal his feelings right away. You kind of have to drag that stuff out of him."

"I guess that's true. He doesn't talk much about his past. Should I be concerned about anything else?"

"Of course not. He's a great guy. He's got his quirks, but I'm sure you've figured them out already." Rachel smiles.

Linda, feeling so relieved, walks up to Rachel and gives her a warm hug. Rachel didn't expect that kind of reaction, but returns the hug.

"You are staying for the rehearsal, right?" Linda asks as they separate.

"Of course. I cannot stay for the after party, though. In fact, I might cut out before the rehearsal ends, but it would still be nice to see you guys rehearse your ceremony. It would remind me of my own wedding." Rachel presses her lips together in an awkward smile.

"Oh, sure. Maybe one day we might be able to meet you and your husband for dinner sometime," Linda says.

"Yeah, maybe." Rachel reaches for fresh paper towels on the sink to stop the bleeding.

"Can I help you with your forehead? You look like you could use a hand," Linda says.

"Oh no, please, I'll be fine," Rachel lifts her head to stop the bleeding.

Linda grabs her hand and leads her over to the sink. She takes a large hand towel from the basin and begins dabbing Rachel's forehead. "I have five brothers and three sisters. We used to get pretty bloody from time to time. My mom said that I should have become a nurse or a doctor. I used to help mend the kids when they got a little too rambunctious." Linda smiles.

Rachel can't help but like this woman. She seems genuinely sweet and caring. *Brian chose well,* she thinks. "I'm glad Brian is marrying you. I like you, Linda."

Linda's smile widens and she hugs Rachel all over again. She pulls away and hands her the towel. "I like you too, Rachel. I'm sorry but I have to go back to the rehearsal now." She steps back and begins to head out of the bathroom. Before she leaves, she turns back to Rachel. "Any kids?"

"A three year old. His name is Joshua."

"Do you have any pictures?"

"Not on me. I had my purse in the suitcase as well. Wasn't the brightest thing I ever did," Rachel says.

"And probably your wedding ring too?" Linda looks down at Rachel's left hand.

"What?"

"I don't see your wedding ring on. Did you leave that in the suitcase as well?"

"Yes, but I had to. I had that accident and as you can see my hand swelled up quite a bit," Rachel says as she extends her hand to show Linda.

"Oh my God," Linda says, eyeing her very swollen hand. "Are you sure you're alright?"

"I have some pain meds. They make me nauseous, but I'll be alright," Rachel says.

"Is there anything else I can do?" Linda asks.

"No, Linda, I'll be fine. Please, don't worry about me."

"Okay." Linda smiles and walks out of the bathroom.

When Linda finally leaves the bathroom, Rachel's smile immediately reduces to wincing and she begins to get dizzy again. She reaches out with one hand for the bathroom sink to keep from falling. Her knees buckle and she slowly tumbles to the floor. She positions her hands underneath her body and pushes up, but her elbows give way and she falls into a heap. Her face rolls gently to one side of her arm. She tries in vain to keep her head up but the room starts spinning. She closes her eyes to keep from getting nauseous again but soon quietly passes out.

CHAPTER
SIX

I sit on the sofa in my puffy white dress surrounded by relatives speaking in hushed tones. I don't even bother to take the dress off. I paid for it, so I might as well wear it for the rest of the day.

It's drizzling outside. I walk over towards the mudroom, put on my big, clunky rain boots and head out toward my old swing set in the backyard. Fresh air. The weather is a bit warm for the season, but I don't care. I just need a little time to myself.

I sit down gently on the swing to prevent my playground set from collapsing underneath me. I remember when my mom bought it for me. Ted came over to put it together. I think I was about five at the time. I pull back, lift my legs up, and then let the swing do its thing. I'm just swinging, eyes closed, trying not to think about anything.

"Rachel! Come back inside! It's raining, dear!" my mom yells out from the rear porch. I hear her, but I just keep swinging. If I don't say anything, she might just go away. Then I hear the rear door slam shut, and I know that my mother is coming out to talk to me.

She comes up to me carrying my long grey trench coat over her arm. She *drapes the coat over my shoulders and sits on a wooden stump next to the swing.*

I slow my swinging down a bit. "Huh, I thought I got rid of this coat."

"Yeah, I was going to give it away, but I got used to seeing it on you all the time. I never liked that coat, as you know ..." I thought I looked cool in it. It wasn't very girly, but it was warm and functional.

My mom pulls her coat a little tighter. "You never liked the things I bought you anyway." I want to talk about anything other than what happened earlier today. I don't mind talking about the coat, but I know that my mom usually sighs when she's about to change the subject.

Then I hear her sigh.

"Do you want to talk?" she asks.

"Nope, not really," I say. "I just want to be left alone." Usually, when I say something like this, she'll just walk away. She doesn't like getting into big discussions about love and things like that.

I give her a minute, but she doesn't move.

"What Brian did was horrible, without a doubt. I love you very much, and it hurts me to see you go through so much pain. I just want to ask you one question. What is it about Brian that you like so much? I mean, he was always trying to get away from you and most of the time, he wasn't very nice about it."

No one has ever asked me why, including my mom. I have to think about that for a second. I've been in love with Brian for so long that I never even considered anyone else. It has always been him.

I pick up my swinging speed. "Mom, I'm not in the mood to talk."

"No, honey, I'd like to know. You had all of these opportunities to go to college. You gave up Stanford, Yale and Harvard. You're such a beautiful, intelligent young woman, and you gave all of that up for him."

I look down at the dirt. "Only you would ever think that I was beautiful."

"What? Of course you're beautiful! I walked into that living room today and saw a radiant woman looking back at me. You were always pretty, Rachel, but overnight you became this elegant young lady. I'm so proud of you. If Brian can't see that, then it's his loss. He's lucky I don't go out there and kick his ass."

I smile because the only thing my mom kept saying on the way back from church was that she was going to find Brian and kick his ass. I would actually pay money to see that myself. It makes me laugh a little seeing my mom all wound up.

"Mom, I appreciate the fact that you would like to give Brian a beating, but it doesn't matter anymore. You knew he was going to stand me up. I kind of knew as well," I confess.

She reaches over and holds my hand.

"One day you were just friends, then all of a sudden, you were dating each other. Soon after that, you were engaged. It all happened so fast. I definitely didn't see it coming," my mom says.

"Mom, remember senior prom?" I ask.

"What, mine?"

Rachel rolls her eyes. "No, I mean mine, Mom. We're talking about me right now."

"Oh, right, of course. Yes, I remember your senior prom. What about it?

"Remember John Mitchell, the football player that asked me?"

"Oh yeah. I liked him. Very polite kid."

"Well, I never told you this, but there was this contest at the school between the football players to see which one of them could bring the ugliest girl to prom. The jocks would parade us through the night and then their girlfriends would judge the contestants to see who would win. Well, you can say I was one of the ugly girls they were judging."

I never planned on telling my mom about that night. She always gets fanatical about me and I didn't want her to make a scene at the school.

"I'm going to kill that boy!" *she screams. Oh my God. She is losing it.*

"Mom, it's okay," I say as she jumps up from the stump and starts pacing back and forth.

"I'm going to kill this John Mitchell, and then I'm going to take the car and run over the rest of those jerks."

I get up from the swing and grab her arms to calm her down. "Mom! It's all right! It's all right! I didn't know about it until Brian told me," I say. "Mom, *please sit down. Let me finish the story, okay?" My mother huffs a bit longer in a desperate attempt to calm down. Slowly, her breathing returns to its normal pace.*

"You would always tell me that I don't tell you anything about Brian. Well, I am now, here, in the rain, in my wedding dress, telling you everything about him." My mom relaxes her body and she sits back down on the stump. "Remember Brian was dating this girl at school his senior year?"

"Yeah, Tracy Goldman. I never liked her or her mom," Mom says.

"Yes, well, anyway, he was at the prom with Tracy. He found out about the contest and told me what the jocks were up to. I didn't believe him at first, until he made one of the football players confess. Then he took me home. I didn't go inside right away because you might wonder why I came home so early. I just sat out here on the swing waiting for you to go to bed."

I look over at my mom and see a sad look. This must have been hard for her to hear. "I never really had many friends due to my honors classes and hectic academic contest schedule. I went through this 'loner' phase in high school and ended up further isolating myself from everyone. Brian had his own issues, but he managed to have friends. He even ended up having a girlfriend. Even though he struggled through school academically, he found his niche with some kids that were considered outcasts by the popular kids. Nothing Brian wore was either trendy or cool. He had this Beatles-type hairdo and was growing facial hair at the age of fourteen. By the time he was eighteen, he had grown this hideously thin moustache that no matter how he trimmed it, it never looked right. Ted had sent him to driving school when he was sixteen and then all of a sudden he was driving his friends around town. He would be in his 1976 Olds Cutlass packed with his dorky friends, waving to me as I sat at the bus stop. Then the cool kids would drive by and throw donuts at me. What a life."

"Why didn't you tell me any of this before?" my mom asks.

"Wait, there's more," I say.

"Oh my God. Really? I don't think I can take any more of this."

"Mom, let me finish, okay?" I plead.

"Okay."

"When Brian drove Tracy home from the prom, he saw me sitting on the swing out in the yard. After he'd dropped her off, he stopped by to see if I was okay. Then I kind of lost it."

"What do you mean, lost it?" Mom asks.

"I mean, I jumped up and started whaling on him."

"You started hitting him?"

"Yeah. I started hitting him."

"Why?"

"I don't know. He had been so mean to me all these years and now he had the gall to ask me if I was okay. All those years he watched other kids pick on me and did nothing. All those times I would go out of my way to even be friends with him, he would find a way to ditch me. I didn't get it. When did he suddenly start caring about me? So there I was, on top of him, flailing my arms all over his body. He takes hold of my arms and as I was trying to break free to hit him some more, he kissed me."

"What? He kissed you?" Mom asks incredulously.

"He kissed me, and I kissed him right back," I say. "I don't know why I did it, but I did," I say with a smile. I'm sure my mom didn't want to hear all that, but she had to know. She was right. She had no idea how we started dating. I thought the details didn't matter, but it felt good to finally tell someone, especially my mom.

"And then you two started dating?"

"Right after that."

"And then he proposed to you in the yard by the swings. Okay, I can see that now," Mom says. She seems disappointed with the story. I open myself up to her for once but she has this long look on her face. It has been a rough day for her. There is nothing to be happy about.

"Did it feel good to hit him?" Mom asks.

"Yes. I have to say it did feel good. I just couldn't hold it in anymore. It was nice to finally let him have it," I say. He did deserve it. He deserves it now.

"You know, Rachel, this thing with his dad passing ..."

"I know, Mom. I know. He's not quite over it yet. There's no excuse for what *he did, but I knew he wasn't coming. He has this way of giving you clues as to how he's going to act. I knew in my heart that he didn't want to get married. I could have given him more time, but he didn't tell me anything. I wanted him to talk to me about his feelings, about the wedding, his dad, the accident, everything. But he kept it all to himself. He took the easy way out, as usual," I say.*

"Sometimes, the hardest lessons are the best ones." She's right. I would have kept fooling myself for years if this hadn't happened. Now I know what he's capable of doing.

"So what now?" Mom asks.

"I don't know," I say. I never thought it would end this way, but now I have to think about myself for once.

"You never did tell me why you cared about him so much."

"I don't know. There was something inside telling me that one day I was going to marry that boy."

"Was it the time you two met at school?"

"Probably. Well, yes, definitely."

"And you've never felt that for anyone else?" Mom asks.

"Never."

The rain died down, but we stayed out there in the yard just talking. We haven't made time to sit and talk to each other in years. Now here we were, soaked to the bones, talking to each other like we used to do when I was a little girl. It's nice.

RACHEL WAKES up from momentarily passing out on the bathroom floor. Her eyes blink open as she sees the floor from her viewpoint. The room isn't spinning anymore. She puts her hands under her body and eases herself off the ground. Using the sink for support, she slowly pulls herself up and checks her reflection in the bathroom mirror to see if she is bleeding again. She looks a little disheveled, so she runs some water over her face and pats down her hair before stepping out of the bathroom and walking towards the ballroom.

"Rachel." She hears her name being called by a familiar voice and turns around to see Brian hidden in a small cutaway foyer next to the ballroom. She walks over to him and there they stand looking right at each other with no one around.

"Were you looking for me?" Rachel asks.

"I was. Linda told me that she had spoken to you," Brian says.

"Oh, I see …" Rachel shrinks and casts her eyes from side to side.

"Are you alright?"

"Well … not really." Rachel is unsure whether this is the right time to go into the details about her visit.

"Do you need anything?" Brian says.

"No. I just need a little time. No need for your concern. I'm fine," Rachel says as she slowly sits down on a long cushioned bench along the wall next to her. Brian watches and plops on the other bench right across from her.

"You took a long time sitting down," Brian says.

"Yeah. I got into a bit of an accident," Rachel says. "Fender bender. Nothing to worry about."

"Did you go see a doctor?" Brian asks.

"Yeah, yeah, I did all that. Like I said, please don't concern yourself about it." Her harsh tone makes it clear she wants to avoid the subject.

Brian shifts in his seat. "Linda told me that you got married."

"Yeah," Rachel says with a smile. "We got into this conversation about you and me, and then I just kind of blurted it out."

"Wow, Rach. That's such great news. I'm so happy to hear that. You got married." Shock spreads across his face.

"What did you think, Brian? That I would wait for you forever?" Rachel jokingly asks. "There are other fish in the sea, you know."

"No, no. It's nothing like that. I just didn't hear from you for a long time."

"Well, you *did* leave me at the altar."

"I know, I know. It's just that … I don't know. Of course you had to live your life. It's just so nice to hear that you were able to settle down." Brian smiles.

Rachel smirks and looks away. "Oh, by the way, my mom wanted me to tell you that if she sees you again, she's going to kick your ass."

"I don't blame her …"

"She absolutely hates you, Brian." Rachel looks right in his eyes.

"Really? Absolutely hates me? That's pretty strong." Brian squirms a little in his seat.

"You're lucky she didn't hunt you down and stab you or something," Rachel says.

"Wow. Thanks for letting me know." Brian rubs the back of his neck and looks around the foyer. He needs to change the subject because this conversation is going to a place he doesn't want to revisit. He glances at her left hand.

"Where's your wedding ring?" Brian asks.

"I had it taken off. My hand got smashed in the accident. See the tan line?" Rachel lifts up her swollen hand.

"Oh sure. I see it," Brian says.

"Did you think I was lying?" Rachel's eyes narrow as she glares at him.

Brian sputters and shakes his head. "Oh no, I just didn't see it."

Rachel holds his gaze. "You always did have a way of saying something inappropriate."

Brian sits up straighter on the bench and smiles. "Well, after the wedding, maybe we can double date or something."

"Sure, maybe …" Rachel folds her arms.

Brian puts his elbows on his knees and leans into Rachel. He genuinely wants to find out what she's been up to all of these years. "Rachel? How did you know I was here? My mother certainly wouldn't have told you," Brian asks in the nicest way possible.

"I ran into her earlier today by the house. Literally. I almost knocked her down to the ground." Brian's face screws up with worry. "It's not what you think. I simply didn't see her when I was walking past the house. Anyway, I asked about you and she seemed like she was hiding something, so I snuck into your mom's house. I looked around and found an invitation to your wedding in addition to some lovely balloons saying 'Congratulations Brian and Linda.'"

Brian's eyes widen in shock. "Wait. You ran into my mom, asked about me, and then broke into her house?"

"I didn't exactly break in," Rachel says.

"Then what do you call it?" Brian's voice rises in anger.

"I used the spare keys under the plant on the front porch. Look, I gave your mom all the time in the world to say, 'hey, Brian is getting married' or something like that. She looked suspicious and I had to find out why. That's it …" Rachel slightly shrugs.

Brian stands in stunned silence with his mouth wide open. This was the old Rachel he knew so well. He wasn't exactly sure what to say to her, considering what he put her through.

"You got in from the key on the porch," Brian breathes slowly in a desperate attempt to calm down.

"Your mom did change a few things, but not everything. I was surprised to see the keys were still in the same spot where Ted left them," Rachel says.

"She probably forgot that Dad had left a spare set on the porch." Brian turns away to hide his anger at the burglary of his mom's house and her attempt to crash his wedding rehearsal. He needs to find out what she's really up to, and the last thing he wants is a big scene. He takes a breath and turns back with a smile. "You know, Rach, I'm just so glad that you're married. In a way, I'm kind of relieved that you were able to find someone that—"

"You probably thought I was going to come down here and throw myself at you, didn't you?"

"Oh no. That's not what I was saying," Brian quickly responds.

"Make no mistake, Brian, I'm still pretty pissed that you ran off on me on our wedding day, especially now that you are going through with your own wedding to someone else," Rachel says. "So please spare me any kind words, okay?"

Brian sighs and looks directly at his old friend. "I know, I know. I just hope one day you'll get past this anger towards me," Brian says.

"That's never, ever going to happen, Brian. I will go to my grave carrying this anger with me. That was the meanest thing you could have ever done to me, Brian." It feels good to finally say that to him.

"You're right, Rach." Brian hangs his head in complete resignation. She's made her point without making a scene.

"As a matter of fact, what's stopping me from getting up and punching you in the face right now?" Rachel asks.

Brian exhales and shakes his head. "You never read the letter."

"No, Brian. Nothing in that note could have made my life any easier that day," Rachel says.

"You're right."

"You're damn right I'm right, Brian. Let's say I found out that you're getting married from someone else. All right. No big deal. I could have stayed away, let you live your life, whatever. But when I started talking to your mom all of those old instincts and habits came storming back. I knew your mother was lying to me. She didn't have to lie or anything, but her first instinct was to lie to me about you. All I asked her was one simple question: How is Brian? Her lie pulled up every red flag I've ever had with your mother. Now here I am collecting on an old debt you owe me.

"The favor?" Brian asks.

"You got it," Rachel says.

"Rachel, I agree, I do owe you—"

"You owe me so much more than you know."

Brian nods his head and rubs his knees. "And in any other circumstance I would help you, but, Rachel, you haven't even given me a hint of what it is that you want, yet you expect me to stop everything and come with you."

"Yes."

"No, Rach." Brian gets up from the bench. "Any time you think you need to collect on my debt to you, just come see me. Any time except tomorrow," he says turning toward the ballroom.

"We'll see," Rachel says.

Brian stops in his tracks and turns back to her. "What do you mean, *we'll see?*"

"Just what I said, Brian. We'll see."

"When you act like this, you usually do something crazy to get your way."

Rachel throws him an innocent smile. "That's nice. You're making me sound like some crazy person."

"You can be sometimes. I don't remember a time when you didn't get what you wanted," Brian says.

"That's ridiculous." She brushes him off with a flick of her hand.

"It's true. You were always like that. You would ask me to do something, and then I always caved to you. That's why I tried to avoid you, so that I wouldn't be put in that position every single time." Rachel rolls her eyes but he shakes his head. "Not today, Rach. Not today. Do what you want, Rachel. I'm done being afraid of you. If you're going to screw up my wedding, then just do it. Get it over with. Ruin my life while you're at it, okay?" Brian says. "Excuse me, but I have guests waiting for me." Brian storms off to the ballroom.

Rachel remains seated on the bench for a few minutes, recovering from Brian's outburst. She slowly gets up and walks over to the ballroom finding a seat in the back row and sits down. The mood of the wedding party appears relaxed and jovial as they practice their wedding march near the front of the ballroom. Brian and Linda stand in the midst of their friends playfully grooming each other. Jealousy washes over Rachel as she tries to remember the few times that Brian seemed happy while in a relationship with her. Even though those moments were few and far in between, they reassured her that their past relationship was real and did matter to him.

As she watches him carry on with Linda, she begins to wonder if she and Brian ever loved each other at all. They gleefully teased each other as kids, but that petered out when they got older. Gazing at the happy couple causes her stomach to flip flop and sends her heart racing. How much more should she endure before revealing the nature of this favor that she needs from Brian? Maybe she should just leave and let Brian start a new life with Linda. She did get to say what she wanted to him. Maybe that's all she needed. She can finally move on and deal with all of the other things by herself.

"Why can't you just let Brian be?" Rachel feels someone step beside her as Mrs. Smith whispers in Rachel's ear. She had just made the decision to leave quietly, when that voice conjures up all the bad feelings she has for Brian and his mother. Now the battle between Mrs. Smith and Rachel rages on.

"I'm not doing anything wrong, Mrs. Smith," Rachel says.

"This is the first time in God knows how long that I can remember seeing Brian this happy. He's gone through so much, on top of losing his dad, and he's finally at a point where he can move on with his life."

"Good for him. Like I said, I'm just sitting here, watching the rehearsal, not bothering anyone."

"What do you think is going to happen here, Rachel? Did you think he was going to leave Linda and come running to you? What more do you want from him?"

Rachel cranes her neck to get a better look at Brian. "He's put on a bit of weight, hasn't he? He looks good. I don't remember him looking so handsome."

Surprised by her candor, Mrs. Smith sits back and softens her tone. "Yeah, I guess you can say he did."

"And a little fitter?"

"They work out together all the time. They are a very active couple," Mrs. Smith says proudly.

"All those pictures in the lobby?" Rachel asks.

"They travel several times throughout the year. The main picture in the lobby was taken in Paris," Mrs. Smith says.

"When did he become a world-class traveler?"

"Ever since they started dating. She's such an outgoing girl, Rachel, and treats him well. No surprises and no drama with that one. I don't think anyone has ever made him that happy. She's genuinely a very nice girl."

"And I guess I wasn't?" Rachel snaps.

"No, Rachel. You have gifts that make you an extraordinary person. Brian never really understood why you cared for him so much. I always wondered about that myself. You two were so different from each other. You had your honors classes and traveled around the country, winning all of those scholastic competitions. You're such an intelligent person, and I have to confess, I was proud of you. You were like a daughter to me, Rachel. But this obsession you have with Brian … You pursued him so long that his father and I accepted the fact you might be able to win him over. His dad always wanted a daughter like you. He adored you so much," Mrs. Smith says.

Rachel sits still in her seat, never turning around to face Mrs. Smith directly. She was right. Mrs. Smith was like a mother to Rachel, but a very strict one. She prevented the children from running around the house and made them do light chores together on the weekends. As the years passed, she treated Rachel with disdain whenever she spent an inordinate amount of time at their house playing with Brian. Rachel never disrespected or disobeyed her when she was a young girl, but she did find ways around Mrs. Smith to get what she wanted. That unique trait aggravated Mrs. Smith, but she tolerated Rachel for Brian's sake. They stopped liking each other years ago, but they did have respect for one another.

Rachel turns around to Mrs. Smith and leans over to her. "Brian and I are clearly over. That part of our life is gone. You're absolutely right, Mrs. Smith. I never made him that happy."

A wan smile emerges on Mrs. Smith's face as she leans back into her chair. They both sit in silence for a few seconds.

"I have so many pictures of you and Brian laughing together when you two were kids. I pulled out the photos the other day as I was getting some old pictures of him for the photomontage at the reception. Looking through those, I can't help but get a little emotional. It was such a happy time for all of us," Mrs. Smith says.

Rachel nods her head. "It's too bad you and Mom stopped getting along."

"That's one of the most tragic parts in all of this. I miss your mom, but sometimes these things just happen over time," Mrs. Smith says.

"Yeah. Life just happens, right?" Rachel turns and looks directly at Mrs. Smith. "You just never think loved ones could hurt you so badly that it changes your view of the world forever. It took years, Mrs. Smith, to get over everything. Slogging through grief for months brought me to the lowest point in my life, but what could I do about it? Die?"

"Die? That's a little extreme, Rachel," Mrs. Smith says.

"Unfortunately, that's what it felt like," Rachel responds as she turns back around.

Mrs. Smith shakes her head dismissively. "Rachel, I never took you for someone who would let your emotions get the best of you."

"I'm only human, Mrs. Smith." Rachel says.

Mrs. Smith places a hand on Rachel's shoulder. "You were like my daughter, Rachel. Sometimes, I would like to think you still are."

"And Linda?" Rachel challenges.

"She's family now. I hope to see grandkids sooner than later. Then maybe I can do right for them that I couldn't do for you."

"For me?"

"I never thought I could do anything to make you leave my heart. I wish I had done things differently. I do love you, Rachel. I'm sorry that I never told you that," Mrs. Smith says.

"It wouldn't have changed anything, Mrs. Smith."

They both watch the rehearsal in silence.

"Look at him, Rachel," Mrs. Smith says. "He's a different person. I can finally see my young boy again. It's been so many years. I never thought I would see that side of him again."

"It is nice to see that too," Rachel admits.

"Let him be happy, Rachel. Please. Just let him marry this wonderful girl."

Rachel has never heard Mrs. Smith plead for anything. With unrequited love, her greatest adversary sits behind her begging for her son's happiness and freedom. Her body relaxes in complete surrender. It is time to move on.

"Okay. You win," Rachel says as she turns completely around to face Mrs. Smith. "I'll leave."

Mrs. Smith's face breaks into the widest smile she has ever seen on that woman. "Thank you so much." She leans in to give Rachel a kiss on the cheek and rises to join the wedding rehearsal.

The event planner rallies members of the wedding party into the starting configuration for the procession. Rachel prepares to leave but waits for them to walk through their rehearsal. First Brian proceeds down the aisle, then the bridesmaids, followed by Linda walking arm in arm with her parents on each side. When they reach the end of the aisle, Linda takes her place next to Brian and hooks her arm into his. Watching this happy scene is too much for Rachel to bear. She realizes that Brian will not come to her aid and that she needs to complete her mission all by herself. Asking him for help on his wedding day seemed illogical at best and Rachel had no right to ask him to do such a thing. She knows it's time to leave.

She stands up, turns away from the party, and heads down the aisle towards the ballroom doors, stopping in the middle of the aisle to have one last look before she departs. Brian and Linda give each other that look that only lovers give—two people beginning their long journey of life together. Rooted to her spot, Rachel drinks in this image of happiness and pure joy.

Waking from her delirium, she eases her way backwards down the aisle toward the exit. She trips on a chair, loses her footing, and tumbles back onto a row of chairs, landing on the floor.

Lying on top of the chairs, arms and legs akimbo, she listens to the silence fill the ballroom. Through the legs of fallen chairs, she can see everyone in the room turn towards her contorted body to see what happened. Everyone stands still, frozen, watching her tangled mess. No one comes to help Rachel up off the floor.

Rachel starts having flashbacks of all the times she fell down in front of others while growing up: the 4th Grade Spelling Bee Championship, the Junior

Chess Championship (on TV), both grade school and high school graduations, every sport she had ever played, in the hallways at school, the cafeteria, and junior and senior prom. Her tall, slender figure and large feet made it difficult to walk gracefully. After each time she fell, she could always hear people gasping and laughing at her. She learned to laugh at herself the loudest to make it seem like it never bothered her. But it always did.

Using her arms, Rachel pushes herself off the floor. As she struggles to get up, she can hear all of those familiar sounds: the gasps, the laughter, the giggling. She manages to rise from the gnarled heap and sees everyone in the room gawking and laughing at her. Rachel stands there completely still for a few moments then turns toward Brian and screams.

"All I ever wanted you to do was one favor for me! I've never, ever asked you for anything else and all you can do is stand there and laugh at me? I needed you to help me! I've always helped you, Brian. And you've never done anything to help me. Ever!"

Sobs wrack her body as Rachel struggles to control her emotions. Brian never laughed when she fell down in the aisle, but he had laughed at her in he past. There was a time during junior high when he and his friends would trip her between classes and laugh uproariously. It was his desperate attempt to push her away and create some emotional distance. She never forgot that and always carried that pain with her.

"Did your mom ever tell you I was there when the doctors sent you home to die after the accident? I stayed in that bed with you the whole time. Do you remember when you went back to school and everyone started picking on you? I stuck up for you every single time someone teased you about the accident or gave you a hard time. Did any of that mean anything to you?! Huh, Brian?!"

As she continues her verbal assault, blood starts trickling down Rachel's face. The fall reopened her head wound, but does nothing to slow down her tirade.

"Goddammit, Rachel!" screams Mrs. Smith as she storms up the aisle gearing for a fight. As the older woman verges upon her, Rachel pulls back her hand and SMACKS her face with all of her might. Mrs. Smith falls back from the blow. Rachel stands there in complete shock, her hand stinging. She didn't even realize she slapped Mrs. Smith until she saw her stumble back away from her.

Everyone gasps and the room goes completely quiet.

"That's for slapping me on my wedding day!" Rachel roars at Mrs. Smith and directs her anger towards the others in the room. "Who the hell slaps a girl on her wedding day?! Really?!"

She stops yelling and takes a moment to see all of the eyes staring at her. No one makes a sound. Her heart beats wildly in her chest as she hears herself breathing. Rachel, with blood all over her face, begins to walk backwards towards the exit.

"Brian, I am so sorry. I tried to be good. I'm so sorry," Rachel mutters as tears roll down her face. She then turns away and begins to run out of the ballroom. Brian finally leaps forward and runs towards his mom still in shock from the slap. He checks her over to make sure she is okay and bolts after Rachel.

"Rachel! Wait!" Brian yells, but Rachel runs out of the ballroom with Brian on her heels. She sprints to the elevator, but the doors do not open quickly enough. Spinning around, she finds the set of escalators on the other side of the foyer. She runs towards them and races down the stairs. Brian dashes into the foyer, but misses Rachel and follows right behind. Rachel makes it down to the lobby, runs right past the hotel guests, and heads out through the doors. Brian reaches the lobby as well, but due to the crowd of people milling around the entrance, he loses sight of her. He frantically asks people if they had seen anyone fitting Rachel's description.

Rachel walks through the blowing snow down the street that takes her to the bridge looking over the river. She runs up to the center of the bridge but encounters a barrier blocking foot traffic as construction workers make evening repairs on the bridge. Rush hour traffic prevents her from running across to the other side of the bridge.

"Rachel!" Brian runs up the walkway of the bridge to catch up to her. She tries in vain to find another way around. With no other option, she crawls under the barrier and races through the bright construction lights and around the maze of workers, welders, and drillers.

"Rachel! Stop! You're not supposed to be in there!" Brian screams as she continues through the construction site. With the lake effect snow, the blood and tears in her eyes, and the construction lights, she has difficulty seeing where she is going. She can hear construction people telling her to stop, but she continues to run.

A large steel beam being lifted from a crane cuts her off. When she tries to get around the beam, she slips on the wet snow, tumbles forward, and hits the steel beam smack-dab on her forehead. With no railing on the walkway, she careens off the bridge and falls thirty feet into the river.

Rachel hits the water hard driving her in and out of consciousness. She ingests water as she struggles to reach the surface of the freezing river. With every breath she takes to keep herself from drowning, she hears Brian yelling out for her. Her body goes into shock and slowly stops struggling to survive. She takes one last gasp of air and sinks into the water. As Rachel plunges to the bottom of the river, she sees the light above her fading away.

With no air left in her lungs, she gurgles out one more cry. "Mommy! Mommy!!"

Rachel closes her eyes and loses consciousness one last time.

"MOMMY! MOMMY!" *I yell as I run through the bright morning light from the yard towards the house. I stop at my back porch and wait for my mom to answer me.*

"Rachel?" my mom calls. I stand as still as a stone, trying to contain my excitement. Then, without waiting a second more, I burst into the house.

The sun beams into our happy home. Sheer red curtains flutter in the air as a gentle spring breeze flows through every open window. I can smell the bread my mom is baking in the oven, just for me. I can hear those sweet chimes ringing softly throughout the house with every puff of air.

"Mommy?" I call again. Sneaking around the kitchen, I look for her. I hold firmly to some daisies that I picked from the yard, especially for her. I'm wearing my favorite pink summer dress, trying to find her before she finds me. Mom likes to hide so she can jump out and surprise me with tons of hugs and kisses. With the brightest grin that I can hardly contain inside my heart, I quietly move from the kitchen to the living room.

All of a sudden my mom grabs me from behind, picks me up, and twirls me around. She kisses me all over making me laugh uncontrollably.

"I got you, sweetie!" she cries out with a beautiful smile as she dances me around the room, holding me tightly around her waist.

"I love you, baby," my mom whispers.

"I love you too, Mommy," I whisper back into her ear. I make her giggle as I nibble on her earlobe. We are both trying to make each other laugh, but then my mom slows down to embrace me firmly.

"You know what, sweetie?"

"What, Mommy?" I ask. She doesn't respond. I ask her again, but she says nothing. She just holds me tightly. I kiss her ear and as I close my eyes I smell the bread from the kitchen. "Can I have some bread now, Mommy?"

"Of course."

Then I close my eyes, letting her hair drape across my face, as she waltzes me around the room.

CHAPTER
SEVEN

Rachel quickly comes to. She coughs up water from her lungs as she struggles to breathe. A large, bearded man takes her hand from her chest and leans over her.

"Are you okay, lady?" the bearded man asks. Rachel is still gasping for air as a couple of other men drape blankets over her cold body. "You might want to get out of those wet clothes when you get the chance."

As she tries to figure out where she is, Rachel musters the strength to sit up. The men are all dressed in heavy coats and waterproof boots.

"Where am I?" Rachel asks the bearded man.

"City of Chicago Cleaning Barge. We were going down the river when you fell in. One of the guys couldn't tell it was you, but said he saw something fall in from the bridge. You're lucky we were able to pull you in quickly. You were a good thirty feet down when we finally got to you."

One of the workers comes in with an oversized pair of pants and a shirt for Rachel to wear. The men look away as she grabs the clothes and begins to change under the blankets. She can't see very well without her glasses and struggles to focus on everything around her.

"The construction workers on the bridge told us that you ran through the construction barrier, slipped, and fell in," the bearded man says. "That's why the barrier is there, ma'am. You're lucky you didn't get yourself killed."

"Yeah, I suppose so." Rachel stammers through chattering teeth. She wraps the blankets around her clothed body.

"And she's alive!" The bearded man yells out. The crew in the boat yells out in excitement. "The Coast Guard and the Police boat are heading this way. Should be here any minute now, missy. They're going to take you to the hospital to have you checked out." He begins to put his first aid kit away.

"Well, thank you for rescuing me from the water," Rachel says.

"Well, we got you out of the water but we weren't the ones that pulled you from the bottom."

"Then who did?" Rachel asks.

"Some guy jumped into the water from the bridge. He's in the other compartment right now." Just as he stops speaking, Brian enters the compartment from the other room, covered in blankets as well.

"Brian?"

"Rachel." Brian stops mid-step when he sees his old friend. They hold each other's gaze for a moment.

The bearded man looks from one to the other. "So you two know each other?" he asks, smiling.

"You can say that," Rachel says.

Brian walks over and sits across from Rachel. "Excuse me, sir, do you mind if I have a minute alone with her?"

"Just as long as the young lady is okay with it."

"Yes, that's fine," Rachel says.

"Okay then. I'll be up on deck. You know, you might not have that much time. The Coast Guard should be arriving any minute now." The bearded man gets up and walks out of the compartment leaving Rachel and Brian alone.

"When did you learn how to swim?" Rachel splutters.

"I took lessons a few years ago," Brian says. "Did you ever end up telling anyone?"

"Tell anyone about what?" Rachel asks.

"That you saved me that day at the lake," Brian says.

"It wasn't that big a deal, Brian. You would have done the same for me."

They both know that Rachel saving Brian from drowning at the lake was a very big deal; it was something they never talked about … until today.

"Rachel, is it too late for me to say *thank you* for saving me at the lake?"

"You saved me today, didn't you?" Rachel attempts a half smile while trembling. "That should make us even, right?"

"I guess so," Brian says. Rachel begins to wince in pain. "Are you okay?"

"Not really. I don't know what just happened," Rachel says.

"You fell into the river from the bridge …"

"Yeah, I get that, but how did all of this …" Rachel starts, but she has to stop talking due to a pounding headache. She closes her eyes and puts her hand on her head.

"Rach, are you alright? Do you need me to bring the Captain back out?"

"No. I'll get through it," Rachel says. She reopens her eyes and looks over at Brian. "Oh no. Your rehearsal."

"Uh, yeah," Brian says.

Rachel remembers what happened at the hotel. "Oh, Brian. I am so sorry." She looks away from him in shame. "I promised you I wasn't going to be any trouble and I ended up ruining your day."

"Yeah. You slapped Mom." He's trying to look serious, but then he begins to chuckle quietly. "You actually slapped her. Wow."

"Oh my God. I did slap your mom … in front of everyone," Rachel says. "Oh man. I don't know what possessed me …"

"Was it true what you said, that she slapped you first?" Brian asks.

"Yeah. You weren't really supposed to know that."

"Why did she slap you?"

"Brian, I don't know. You didn't show up. She came to give me your letter. I said something stupid, then she slapped me."

Although Brian thought it was comical that Rachel slapped his mom at the rehearsal, Rachel thinks the slap was a culmination of many bad things that happened between her and Brian. None of it had to happen, but she does not think the whole slapping episode was funny at all.

Brian slowly realizes from Rachel's sad demeanor the seriousness of what had happened. "Rachel, I'm the one who should apologize. Not only for standing you up, but also for not making time to talk to you about my feelings about the wedding, about my Dad, about everything," Brian says. "That was wrong of me, and whatever I was going through I should not have taken my anger out on you."

Rachel looks over at Brian and for the first time in many years, she can finally see sincerity in him. Here he is making amends for the things he had done to her.

"Okay. Well, now what?" Rachel asks.

"Well, first of all, we need to take you to the hospital," Brian says.

"No, Brian. About you and me? About us? About everything?" Rachel asks.

"There were things you needed to say to me, right? Did you say everything that needed to be said?"

Rachel has to think about that question. "I think so," she says. "I had other things going on, Brian. I found out that you were getting married and I said to myself, 'How dare he?' So I went on a mission to find you. I had to tell you— wait, no, I had to *show* you how painful it was for me when you left me at that church after all that we had been through."

"I can see that now, Rachel," Brian says. He does not believe the entire episode has resolved itself but for now it looks like everything might be forgiven, if only for tonight.

"Was it true what you said? You came over to the house when the doctors sent me home that night?" Brian asks.

Rachel sits up and looks over at Brian to see if he was ready to hear about a time in his life that he doesn't remember. "I snuck out of the house the night the hospital had dropped you off. I made my way across the street, in my pajamas, of course, and headed to the house. The front door was left open, for some reason.

From the front porch, I could see your parents in the living room talking with a couple of doctors and nurses. I opened the front door, snuck past everyone in the living room, and went upstairs to your bedroom. You were lying so still with all these tubes connected to you. I crawled into your bed and stared at you for a time. I could only see your closed eyes since you had that mask covering most of your face. All of a sudden, you opened your eyes. You took one look at me and then started to smile. I brought all of my stuffed animals to play with you. They were my *buddies* that we used to play with whenever you came over, remember?" Brian nods patiently.

"Well, eventually, your parents came in and saw me playing on your bed. Your mom tried to pull me out of your bed, but I started crying and screaming. My mom came running up the stairs to your bedroom. She saw what was happening and grabbed your mom trying to get her to let go of me. They got into this big argument and as that was happening the doctors finally noticed you had just woken up. You had been in a coma after the accident, Brian. The doctors were never able to wake you up during recovery. The first time you woke up was when I crawled into your bed.

"Everyone was so happy you were finally awake. Your mom and dad just smothered you with kisses. The doctors wanted to take you back to the hospital, but your mom said no. Whatever was going to happen to you that night, it was going to happen at home, with your family by your side. Your mom let me stay and we ended up playing throughout the night. You were so weak, but you could move your hand a little bit here and there. You couldn't talk because they kept the oxygen mask on, but I understood you. Our parents stayed awake all night to keep an eye on your progress. We played until we both fell asleep. Then my mom picked me up from your bed and carried me home."

Brian was never told about Rachel coming down to the house that night. It took at least a couple of years for Brian to fully recover from the accident. He doesn't even remember the accident, or the first couple of months after waking up from his coma. The hospital had sent Brian home to die in peace that night, but he pulled through.

The boat slows down and bumps against the pier. Through the porthole they see flashing lights as the Coast Guard waits for them at the dock. Brian rises from his seat and Rachel tries to follow suit, but falls back down to her chair.

"Rach, just stay here until they come and take you to the hospital," Brian says.

"Okay. As soon as they take me, you should jump in a cab and head back to the hotel."

"Oh no, I'm going with you." Brian pulls his blanket around his body resolutely and sits back down.

"No, Brian, I've made a mess of things today. I'll be fine," Rachel says.

"As soon as I know you are okay, then I'll leave. I just want to make sure you make it there all right," Brian says.

Rachel isn't in the position to argue. She agrees. Brian watches Rachel as she closes her eyes and leans back against the wall.

"Rachel? Why did you care about me so much?"

Rachel's eyes pop open and she turns away from him slightly. "Brian, I don't think this is the right time."

"I know, but man, Rachel. All those times I was so mean to you, yet you always came back. I don't know. Why did you keep coming back—"

Rachel quickly interrupts. "It's just this thing that happens, Brian! It's this thing that happens when you know you're going to care for somebody for the rest of your life. From the moment I met you, I knew it. I just knew it. I can't explain. You just know. Your heart knows. And those feelings stay with you forever, no matter what," Rachel says.

They can hear the commotion of emergency workers entering the boat.

"Your husband will be glad to know that you're okay," Brian says.

Rachel looks away as the emergency team enters the compartment. "Yeah," Rachel says quietly.

"Rachel, you never told me your husband's name …"

The medical team cuts him off to care for Rachel. Other emergency team members examine Brian at the same time. Several ambulances and fire trucks are there to greet them at the dock. The paramedics place Rachel in the ambulance and treat her head wound and hypothermia. Brian gives his side of the story to the police in the other ambulance as the emergency personnel treat him for hypothermia as well.

Brian observes a paramedic tending Rachel's wounds as he relays the details of the accident to the police. As the police take his statement, he watches the awkward exchange between Rachel and the paramedic.

"Have we met before, miss? You seem very familiar," the paramedic says.

"No. I don't know you, sorry." Rachel looks away.

"Are you sure? You just seem so familiar," he asks again.

"No, I don't know you. I don't even live here," Rachel insists.

Brian overhears the puzzling conversation. A guy might use that line of questioning to get a girl's phone number, but this was different. He seemed to recognize her in a more significant way.

"And you said your friend ran through the construction barrier and then fell in the river," one of the two police officers asks. Brian is distracted as he sees Rachel looking uncomfortable with her treatment from the paramedics in the other ambulance.

"Mr. Smith?" one of the police officers says as they try to get his attention.

Brian turns around and faces the police officers again. "Uh, yes. Yes. She ran past the barrier."

"Do you know why she ran past the construction barrier?" the officer asks.

"She attended my wedding rehearsal at the hotel by the bridge. She got upset and ran off. She headed to the bridge trying to get away," Brian says.

"You said she was upset?" the officer asks.

"Yeah, she and my mother got in an argument, then she ran out."

"Mr. Smith, we had other officers obtain statements from the people on the bridge, trying to piece together what had happened. We suspect that your friend Rachel was trying to commit suicide," the officer says.

Brian recoils in shock and anger. "Suicide? No, no. She simply made a bad decision by going through the construction barrier. I saw her get hit by a moving steel beam that pushed her off the bridge. If the railing had still been up, she would not have fallen in the river. Yes, it was a mistake on her part, but she is definitely not suicidal."

The thought of her doing anything to harm herself is inconceivable to him. She had gone through a lot in life, but she doesn't think like that. She was never a quitter. She would fall down while playing baseball or soccer, but she would always get back up. She even fell on national TV, brushed herself off, and walked across that stage to receive her trophy. She always got back up. It was like she was performing a very complicated dance move. Falling and rising became her niche. In spite of her academic success in high school, she was voted "Most Likely to Fall and Get Back Up." The kids used to tease her, but it didn't seem to bother her. *But it did. It did bother her,* Brian thinks.

"If we interview your friend is she going to tell us the same thing?" one of the officers asks.

"Yes. Absolutely."

"Regardless of what happened, you did a very brave thing jumping in the river and rescuing your friend."

"Well, I had to. She did the same for me years ago when we were kids."

"Really?" the officer asks.

"Yeah. We were best friends," Brian says.

"Hmm. It just seemed that once she hit the water, she sank to the bottom almost immediately. She didn't try to surface at all," the officer says.

"She must have hit the water awkwardly. Or it might have been due to the accident," Brian says.

"Accident?" the officer asks.

"Yeah. She said she got into some car accident recently. She has some kind of head wound and her hand looks pretty swollen."

The officer looks over at his partner. "Oh, we didn't know that. That might explain things a bit." He closes his logbook and glances at the other police officer interviewing Rachel.

"Thank you for your time. We'll call you if we need anything else," the other officer says. The officers walk away from the ambulance. Brian tries to get up, but one of the paramedics stops him.

"Sorry, sir. We're taking you to the hospital now," the paramedic says.

"No, I'm alright. I want to ride in the other ambulance with Rachel." As soon as he says this, the rear doors in the other ambulance close and the vehicle speeds off. Brian tries to break away from the paramedic but it's too late. "Where are they taking her?"

"They're heading to Northwestern Emergency Center. You can check up on her when we arrive," the paramedic says. As the paramedic lowers Brian back down to the gurney, a cab rushes up to the ambulance. The car door flies open and out jumps Linda.

"Brian! Oh my God!" Linda screams as she rushes over to Brian. She throws her arms around his neck as he looks over to see the ambulance carrying Rachel drive away. "The police told me you two fell into the river."

"No. Rachel slipped and fell into the river. I jumped in to save her," Brian says.

"Rachel fell in and you jumped in after her?" Linda pulls back and looks Brian in the eyes.

"Yeah. She fell in and sank straight down to the bottom. I couldn't wait for help, so I jumped."

"Is she alright?"

"Yeah. They're treating her right now." Brian says.

Linda seems concerned about Rachel, but doesn't ask anything more about her. "Are *you* okay, honey?"

"A little cold, but I'm fine."

One of the paramedics interjects. "Sir, we do have to take you to the hospital."

"I'm okay, I'm okay," Brian says. "I don't need to go to the hospital. I'm fine."

Linda jumps in. "I'm his fiancée, sir. I can take him back to the hotel and get him warmed up."

"What's going on?" the other paramedic in the driver's side of the ambulance asks as he peers his head out of the window.

"He's refusing to go to the hospital," the paramedic replies to his partner and turns to Brian. "We checked you out and you seem fine. No obvious injuries. Usually we try to have you checked out at the hospital anyway, but if you are refusing care ..."

"I'll take care of him," Linda says. "If anything comes up, we'll go to the emergency room."

"Alright, then." The paramedic jumps into the rear of the ambulance and closes the back doors.

As the ambulance takes off, Linda hugs Brian one more time. "Are you sure you're alright?"

"Yeah," Brian says.

"Brian, I need to know what's going on. Rachel said your mom slapped her on her wedding day. Why would she do something like that? If your mom knew about her wedding, why didn't you know she had gotten married?"

Brian's shoulders sag and he shakes his head. This is it.

"Linda, there's so much I need to tell you, but not here. I know I'm asking a lot, but I need to check on Rachel in the hospital. She's not acting right. Something's wrong."

Linda takes a deep breath to calm herself. "Brian, was she awake when they put her in the ambulance? Were they able to revive her?"

"Yeah."

"Then she will be okay." She pulls him closer. "We're getting married tomorrow and I have lots of questions about you and Rachel. This woman shows up, out of the blue, hits your mom, and ruins our wedding rehearsal. Clearly, she's not well but I want to salvage what's left of this night. I don't think that's too much to ask. She needs help. She was bleeding all over herself even before she fell into the river. Let the doctors and nurses take care of her. Please."

Brian can't help but remember Rachel's behavior when the paramedics treated her. She kept shaking her head and pushing them away when they tried to examine her head wound. He wants to see if she is okay, but he knows Linda is right. There isn't much more he can do.

"Okay," Brian says.

"Good. Let's go," Linda says as they enter the cab. They head back to the hotel.

Two hours later Brian sits among family and friends in the extravagant wedding suite at the hotel. The conversation with Linda went better than expected, especially when he talked about the impact of his dad's death on him. She was shocked that he stood Rachel up at the altar, but she understood. She was more upset that he didn't trust her enough to tell her about his past, including his relationship with Rachel. He promised to tell her everything going forward. *She is way too good for me,* he thinks.

Their guests laugh and drink the night away while he ponders the state of his friend's health. He watches Linda dance around with her friends while his mom laughs off the crazy night with his future in-laws. Brian tries to enjoy himself but his mind keeps wandering back to Rachel.

He keeps reliving the rescue in his head.

I see her go over the barrier and then into the river. As soon as she hits the water, she quickly begins to sink. I yell out for Rachel, who looks as if she is not even trying to stay afloat. I shout for help, but it doesn't look like she has much time. The construction workers scramble to find anything to help get her out of the water, but I can't wait. I've never jumped into a body of water that high before, but I don't hesitate. I watch her plummet to the bottom and jump right in.

Hyperventilating for a moment, I fight through the cold water. Once in, I look for Rachel. Nothing. I scream her name as the construction workers from up above yell and point to the last spot they saw her in the water. Swimming over to that position, I take a deep breath and dive into the dark waters. I look through the cold water for a few seconds, see nothing, and come back up. One more time. I take a much deeper breath and go down again, swimming as far as I can. High-powered beams of light pierce the water as construction workers aid in the effort of retrieving Rachel.

I'm about to resurface when a shaft of light hits something right below me. With whatever air left in my chest, I sink deeper with my arms outstretched. Just when I think my chest might burst from lack of air, I grab hold of something heavy. Pulling it with every bit of strength, I kick up to the surface. We emerge from the water. The sounds of cheers echo through the walls of the riverbank as a rope falls right next to me. I grab on and wrap my other arm around Rachel's neck to keep her head out of water. A minute later, the tugboat pulls right up to us.

Linda interrupts Brian's thoughts as she gives him another beer and a kiss. She caresses his cheek softly and waltzes over to another group of merrymakers. A couple of hours later, the party finally ends. With everyone out of the suite, Brian and Linda get ready for bed. Wearing his pajamas, Brian sits on the bed and watches the snow drift gently on skyscrapers and high rises throughout the city. He walks out to the balcony and takes in the beauty of the city landscape in the dead of night. He glances over to the bridge where Rachel almost lost her life.

The most troubling aspect of this night was the way Rachel ran past that construction barrier. Rachel was very stringent about rules, never the big risk taker and always followed the letter of the law. He can only remember a handful of times when she strayed from the norm. Then he kept thinking about that favor she wanted him to do. Everything Rachel did today was so out of character and made very little sense. Maybe his pending nuptials triggered old memories of what he did to her and sent Rachel on a downward spiral. Brian feels a bit responsible for that. He could never blame her for acting like she did today. Guilt washes over him as he ponders the fate of his friend.

"Brian, honey? I think I left one of my bags in the ballroom. It had some of my night stuff in it, like my curling iron and slippers. Can you go down and see if it's there?" Linda asks from the bathroom. Lost in his thoughts, Brian does not hear a word from his fiancée. Stepping out of the bathroom she sees Brian out on the balcony. She walks up to him and he wraps his arms around her.

"Isn't it a beautiful night?" she asks.

"Hmm. A bit cold though," Brian says as he looks back out to the snow-covered city.

"Did you hear me earlier? Can you do me a favor?"

A few minutes later, Brian strolls into the ballroom and turns on the lights. Wearing jeans and a T-shirt, he spots the bag next to the back row of chairs and proceeds towards it. As he closes the distance, he hears a cell phone ring. He turns towards the sound trying to locate the phone. He finds it plugged into a wall-charger by the entrance. Unplugging the cracked phone, he looks down at the number and opens the flip phone to answer the call.

"Hello?" Brian answers. He hears the voice of a frantic woman trying to get a hold of Rachel and immediately recognizes the owner. "Ms. Stein, it's me. Brian." He hears her talk for a few moments, and then Brian's expression goes from curiosity to concern. "Ms. Stein, she's at Northwestern Hospital. She had a bit of an accident. She seems fine—" Brian says, but he doesn't get to finish his sentence as he hears something unexpected from Ms. Stein.

"Wait. What? What happened?" Brian asks.

CHAPTER
EIGHT

Rachel sleeps in a small, draped-off section of the emergency room at Northwestern Hospital. After stabilizing her condition, the doctors let her rest in the ER until a room opens up. She slowly begins to wake up and hears people bustling around the emergency room. A minute later a doctor and one of the nurses pull back the curtains around her bed.

"Good evening, Ms. Stein," the doctor says. "My name is Dr. Owen. I wanted to see how you were doing." The nurse checks her vitals as Dr. Owen looks over her chart.

"My head's killing me," Rachel says as she tries to sit up. Dr. Owen puts his hand on her shoulder.

"Please, don't try to get up. You have a pretty bad cut on your forehead, along with some bruising around the area. Plus, we noticed that your left hand is swollen so we took some X-rays and discovered a compound fracture in your hand. Results regarding your head injury came back negative. When we first examined you, we thought there were complications due to hypothermia but quickly detected the other injuries. We obviously want to keep you here overnight. Later this evening, we'll put a cast on your hand, and then we'll check out everything else. We anticipate that if everything clears up, we can let you go in the morning," Dr. Owen says.

"No, doctor. I need to get out of here," Rachel mumbles to Dr. Owen.

"Sorry, Ms. Stein. Considering what happened when you went into the water, we definitely have to keep you overnight. Those injuries that you sustained when you fell over will need to be monitored, at least for the next twelve hours." Dr. Owen bends down toward Rachel. "Ms. Stein? You did sustain these injuries as you fell in the water, is that correct?

"I think so," Rachel replies reluctantly. "I don't know."

"Do you not recall how you received the other injuries? Did you fall on the bridge before you went in? Did you fall on something in the water?"

Rachel evades his line of questioning. An ER nurse passes Rachel's room and stops mid-step to do a double take. She walks back to the door, stares at Rachel, and walks right in.

"Mrs. Matheson? Is that you?" the ER nurse asks. Rachel looks at the nurse who just called her by her married name. She immediately sits up. "What are you doing here, Mrs. Matheson?"

"Nurse? This is not Mrs. Matheson. It's Ms. Stein. We just admitted her a few hours ago. She fell into the river and we're just going over her condition ..." Dr. Owen says to the ER nurse. The ER nurse looks at Rachel for a few moments. Rachel tries to look away hoping the nurse does not recognize her.

"Doctor, may I speak to you for a moment?" the ER nurse asks.

"Yes, of course." He turns toward Rachel. "Ms. Stein, I'll be right back. Just lie down and relax. We'll get you to your room shortly."

Dr. Owen and the ER nurse step away from Rachel's station and walk a few steps down the hallway. Rachel can see them talking to each other. She knows that ER nurse; she was the one that admitted her last time. Rachel panics, knowing that the nurse will tell Dr. Owen all about Rachel and what happened to her.

A large commotion can be heard down the hallway of the ER. Several gurneys are being wheeled in with a mass of paramedics, fire department medics, police, and ER staff. It looks like a few people are being wheeled into the emergency room.

"All hands! The bus accident is here!" one of the ER technicians yells out. All of the ER nurses and doctors rush to tend the new patients, including Dr. Owen and the ER nurse that recognized Rachel.

Rachel takes full advantage of all the chaos and plans her getaway. She doesn't want to get trapped in the hospital. She wants to leave. Now.

Sitting up, she uses all her strength and manages to roll out of the emergency room bed. Standing in her patient smock, she glances around the room to find her missing clothes. Nothing. She peers into the next station and sees an older woman lying on a gurney with a man sleeping in a chair at the end of the bed. She notices a bag full of clothes sitting on a chair closest to her. Quietly, Rachel leans into the station through the curtain, grabs the bag of clothes, and changes out of her smock into her new attire.

A few minutes later she walks around her station in her stolen clothes. The new outfit hangs a little loose on her, but she thinks she can get through security without gaining any attention. She peeks though the curtain of her station to check for any stray nurses or doctors. Waiting until the coast is clear, Rachel makes her way to the lobby. She walks with her head held high, cool as a cucumber, and makes for the exit. She sees a coat lying on a desk near the security desk, slips it over her arm, and walks right through the door.

On her way out she does not take notice of Brian talking to the admitting staff and security in the lobby. She walks right past him without giving him or anyone else a second glance. While Brian talks to the staff, he thinks he sees someone familiar walking through the hallway towards the exit. He ends the conversation and proceeds to follow the person who just walked out of the ER.

Rachel makes it out of the hospital without getting caught. She walks on the sidewalk, trying get as far away from the hospital as possible. Every few steps she looks over her shoulder to make sure no one is following her. At the end of the block she enters a deserted street next to the hospital. The dark skies fill with drifting snow lightly flowing down through the streetlights, and she can't help but notice all of the snow floating all around her. Rachel walks up to the middle of the street. She wanted to get farther away from the hospital, but decides to stay for a few moments and enjoy the snowfall. She closes her eyes to feel the gentle snowflakes land softly on her face. Then she thinks of Michael and their first date.

An early snow drifts down on a fall evening in Seattle. A young Michael chats with me as he walks me to my car after dinner. I tiptoe precariously in tall heels to a car I parked farther away than I remembered, but it doesn't matter. With my arm wrapped around his, I can hear him talking, but my mind drifts away. I'm falling in love with him, right here, in this moment.

Years pass and I remember sitting by the hospital doors watching Michael pull the car into the hospital driveway. I cradle our swaddled son close to my heart and gaze at the snow falling gently from a dark sky. I rise from the wheelchair, glance up at the sky, and look down at Joshua sleeping soundly in my arms. Dancing a slow waltz in my heart, I kiss him lightly on his soft forehead as my eyes well up with tears. This is my beautiful son.

"Rachel!"

She hears her name and immediately loses her train of thought. Opening her eyes, she slowly turns around. Down the street she spots Brian calling out for her. As soon as Brian starts heading in her direction, Rachel backs up and runs away.

"Rachel, wait! Rachel!" Brian yells as he tries to catch up to her, but she continues to run.

In her weakened condition, her body begins to lose steam and he catches up to her. He keeps his distance as she gives up and stops without turning around.

"You know, don't you?" she says in a soft voice.

"Yes. I know everything. "

"When did you get so smart?" Rachel says with a broken laugh.

"I don't think I can ever be as smart as you," Brian says.

"You're right." She lowers her head. "I didn't want you to see me this way."

"What way?"

"I think you know what I mean."

Brian takes a few steps closer to her. "You came to see me. You came for a reason, right?"

"I don't need you anymore, Brian. Go and get married. She's a nice girl. Don't change things for me. Just let me be, Brian. I don't need any favors from you anymore," Rachel says and starts to walk away.

Brian quietly catches up to Rachel and reaches for her arm. She jerks away from him, but he holds on.

"Let me go, Brian! Let me go!" Rachel screams and tries to pull her hand from his grip.

Brian holds her wrist, tugs her into his chest, and wraps his arms around her.

"What is wrong with you? Let me go! Now!" She yanks away from his chest and decks him in the jaw. He doesn't move and holds her tighter. "Please let me go." She stomps on his foot and knees him in the thigh, and still he holds on.

Feelings rise from her belly. "Get away from me. Please, Brian!" Her resolve shakes and she begins to cry. She falls against his chest and the weight takes both of them down to the ground. The feelings rush out and she sobs uncontrollably.

Brian lets her cry for a few minutes, but eventually she begins to quiet down.

"Don't take me back, please? Don't take me back to the hospital," Rachel says quietly.

"Where you do want me to take you?"

"Take me home."

"But you need to be looked at," Brian says.

"Take me home, okay?" Rachel insists. "Please?"

A few minutes later, Rachel sits in the passenger seat of Brian's car. Not a word passes between them. Brian intermittently glances in her direction, but she soon falls fast asleep. He watches her slumber in awe. Rachel was never one to stay still and quiet, usually laughing, chatting, and moving in her sleep. Now she sits beside him without moving a muscle. This whole day has taken a toll on her. Rachel had been through so much the past few days, and she's done all she could to avoid accepting reality.

As he pulls up to her mother's house, he leans over to wake her and finds her staring through the windshield.

"Rachel?" Brian says her name quietly. She stays silent watching the snow falling down through the evening sky.

"I brought my family down from Seattle to visit my mom a couple of weeks back or whatever. I don't quite remember," Rachel says. "I was driving the rental car when I took my husband and my son downtown for lunch. Not the smartest thing I've ever done. We were in the heart of lunchtime rush." Rachel pauses for a second, then he can hear her beginning to cry. "Brian, I didn't see that truck blow the light. I should have, but it happened so quickly. I saw the truck at the corner of my eye, then there was this bang, then I blacked out. I didn't see what happened to Joshua and Michael. They didn't say a word. They were so quiet. I came to after a few seconds and heard this loud noise coming from somewhere. All I can remember was that I was upside down, bleeding from my head, as I heard men yelling, trying to get us out. I tried looking over to Michael but I could only see a part of him. I couldn't turn to see Joshua. I cried out for both of them, but I blacked out again," Rachel says as she sobs uncontrollably.

Brian didn't want to say it, but he saw the accident after it happened. He was walking to work that day and saw an overturned SUV in the side of the street, completely smashed from one side. The rest of the SUV was a mangled mess. The truck that hit the SUV was totaled and on the other side of the street. There were ambulances and fire trucks everywhere. He stopped for a few moments to see if they were able to pull anyone from the wreckage. He couldn't stay longer than a couple of minutes because he had to get to work. Brian had absolutely no idea she was there, in the car, with her family inside. It was an extraordinary revelation, but he didn't say anything.

"Joshua and Michael?" Brian quietly asks.

"Michael's my husband. Josh is my son. They are supposed to be buried tomorrow, or the next day, I don't know. I was supposed to go to the wake tomorrow, but I can't do it. I can't do it, Brian. I don't want to do it. I can't do it," Rachel says.

"The favor?" Brian asks.

"My mom keeps telling me I have to go see them. I didn't want to. I left the house. I wasn't sure where I was going. Then I ran into your mom. I didn't know I was heading towards your house. I think that's where I was headed. I *was* looking for you, I think. I wanted you to come with me, Brian. I can't do it alone. I can't see them that way," Rachel says as she begins to cry quietly into her hands.

"When did you want to go?" Brian asks.

Minutes later, Brian and Rachel enter the house. Ms. Stein and Aunt Brenda greet Rachel at the door. They take her to her bedroom and lay her down on the bed. Ms. Stein stays with Rachel until she falls asleep. Brian and Aunt Brenda wait in the living room as Ms. Stein returns.

She walks up to her sister. "Can you watch her for a little while?"

"Sure," Brenda says and pats her arm.

Ms. Stein approaches Brian. He gets up from the couch to give her a hug.

"I heard you were getting married tomorrow?" Ms. Stein says as she pulls away.

Brian shakes his head. "She asked me to go with her in the morning. If that's okay with you ..."

"I will take her to the wake, Brian. Don't change your wedding plans because of all this. We never expected this to happen," Ms. Stein says.

"I know, but Rachel's never asked me for anything. I wouldn't even be here if it weren't for her," Brian says.

"You know that's not true, Brian." Ms. Stein says.

"She saved my life, Ms. Stein. More than once, I think. What she's asking me to do is the smallest favor she could ever ask of me," Brian says as tears stream down his face.

"Okay," Ms. Stein says. She gives Brian another hug.

Brian's car pulls up to the driveway of the funeral home. Rachel, dressed in black, sits in the passenger's seat. Rachel's mom stands in the front door with Aunt Brenda, waiting for Rachel to come out so that they can walk in together. Two black hearses sit parked in the driveway waiting to take Joshua and Michael away.

Brian opens his car door, but Rachel grabs hold of his arm.

"I can't do it, Brian. I can't. Please. Take me away. Just drive away, please." Rachel's body shakes as she stifles a sob. Brian holds her hand to comfort her.

"Remember when my dad died? We were in the funeral home. I was in the foyer and I didn't want to go see him. You came up to me and held my hand. Then you walked me inside and remember what you said to me before we went in?" Brian asks.

Rachel shakes her head. "No."

"You told me to just close my eyes if I couldn't take it and imagine something else. Anything else. You know what I imagined?" Brian asks.

"What?"

"When I saw him in that coffin just lying there, so still and quiet, I closed my eyes and imagined he just woke up," Brian says.

"You imagined him waking up?" Rachel asks.

"Yeah. You know, when I was younger, he would pretend to be sleeping, and then he would open one eye and wink at me. Then he would open the other and jump up and hug me. He would make me laugh all the time when he used to do that. I just imagined he was still just pretending. I managed to walk over and kiss him on the cheek, like I did when he took a nap. I said, 'Good night, Daddy.'" Brian says.

"I closed my eyes too that day, Brian," Rachel confesses. "But I don't know if I can do it now."

"You have to say good-bye. If you don't, you'll regret it for the rest of your life. You told me the same thing, and as hard it was, I was glad I had the chance to say good-bye. In my mind, I think he was very happy that I came to see him off," Brian says.

"I think so too," Rachel says.

"I'm here for you, Rachel. Hold on to me for as long as you need to."

"When did you grow up on me, Brian?" Rachel tries to wipe her tears away.

"When I thought I had lost you for good," Brian says. "Never again, Rach."

"The wedding?" Rachel asks.

"I guess this wouldn't be the first time I've stood someone up at the altar," Brian says with a smile. Rachel laughs for a moment.

"You're such a jerk." Rachel snorts.

Brian smiles and watches her for a minute. "You ready?" Rachel nods and puts on her sunglasses.

Rachel, Brian, Ms. Stein, and Aunt Brenda walk into the funeral home parting the crowd of mourners blocking their way. She looks no one in the eye and heads right for the room where Joshua and Michael lie for all to see.

They enter the room, slowly, with one step at a time. Conversations around the room cease as mourners cast sad glances their way. As her loved ones part to make way for her approach, the caskets come in to view. She clutches Brian's hand and her mom's arm, and they begin to walk down the aisle. Rachel's head swoons and her body begins to sway, but she shakes off the fainting spell. She stands up straight and takes a distant look at Joshua and Michael. She closes her eyes.

I open my eyes and immediately I see a bright light shining through the stained glass window in front of the caskets. I let go of Brian and my mom. I'm not afraid anymore. I want to proceed on my own. I go to my sweet Joshua first.

He is lying there in the most beautiful suit he's ever worn. I sneak up to him, like I always did when I would wake him up for breakfast. As I get close he begins to smile.

"Hi, baby," I whisper. "Time to wake up, sweetie." He begins to playfully squirm trying to pretend he's sleeping. I lean over and give him a big kiss. I pick him up and kiss him all over. He tries to giggle his way out of the extra attention.

He laughs, but then he sees the tears flowing from my eyes.

"What's wrong, Mommy?" Joshua asks.

"Nothing, sweetie," I say. "I just love you so much." I continue kissing him all over his face.

With Joshua in my arms, I walk over to Michael. He's already sitting up smiling at me, like the very first day I met him. We walk up to him. He leaps out of his casket and holds my hand. He kisses Joshua on the cheek and then he kisses me.

"I love you, Rachel," Michael whispers.

"I love you too, Michael," I whisper back. He holds me close as I hold on to Joshua tightly, never wanting to let him go ever again. We begin to dance slowly, like a beautiful waltz coming from our hearts. We twirl slowly around the room, face to face, holding each other in a warm embrace. I cry softly, as I gently laugh in joyful bliss. Joshua begins to wipe the tears from my eyes again.

"What's wrong, Mommy?" Joshua asks again.

"Nothing, honey. Absolutely nothing," I say as I kiss him and Michael one last time.

And then she opens her eyes.

Thank you for taking the time to read "The Favor". Please leave a review when you have time. For more information about my next upcoming release, please visit:

www.marcoarodriguez.com

www.ingramcontent.com/pod-product-compliance
Lightning Source LLC
Chambersburg PA
CBHW020541130626
46552CB00012B/1020